T4-AVA-247

Dear Reader,

What could be more romantic than a wedding? Picture the bride in an exquisite gown, with flowers cascading from the glorious bouquet in her hand. Imagine the handsome groom in a finely tailored tuxedo, his eyes sparkling with happiness and love. Hear them promise "to have and to hold" each other forever. . . . This is the perfect ending to a courtship, the blessed ritual we cherish in our hearts. And now, in honor of the tradition of June brides, we present a month's line-up of six LOVESWEPTs with beautiful brides and gorgeous grooms on the covers.

Don't miss any of our brides and grooms this month:

There's no better way to celebrate the joy of weddings than with all six LOVESWEPTs, each one a fabulous love story written by only the best in the genre!

With best wishes,

Nita Taublib

Nita Taublib
Associate Publisher/LOVESWEPT

WHAT ARE *LOVESWEPT* ROMANCES?

They are stories of true romance and touching emotion. We believe those two very important ingredients are constants in our highly sensual and very believable stories in the *LOVESWEPT* line. Our goal is to give you, the reader, stories of consistently high quality that may sometimes make you laugh, sometimes make you cry, but are always fresh and creative and contain many delightful surprises within their pages.

Most romance fans read an enormous number of books. Those they truly love, they keep. Others may be traded with friends and soon forgotten. We hope that each *LOVESWEPT* romance will be a treasure—a "keeper." We will always try to publish

LOVE STORIES YOU'LL NEVER FORGET
BY AUTHORS YOU'LL ALWAYS REMEMBER

The Editors

Gail Douglas
All the Way

BANTAM BOOKS
NEW YORK · TORONTO · LONDON · SYDNEY · AUCKLAND

ALL THE WAY

A Bantam Book / July 1992

If you would be interested in receiving protective vinyl
covers for your Loveswept books, please write to this address
for information:

Loveswept
Bantam Books
P.O. Box 985
Hicksville, NY 11802

ISBN 0-553-44204-X

Published simultaneously in the United States and Canada

Bantam Books are published by Bantam Books, a division of
Bantam Doubleday Dell Publishing Group, Inc. Its trademark,
consisting of the words "Bantam Books" and the portrayal of
a rooster, is Registered in U.S. Patent and Trademark Office
and in other countries. Marca Registrada. Bantam Books, 666
Fifth Avenue, New York, New York 10103.

PRINTED IN THE UNITED STATES OF AMERICA

OPM   0 9 8 7 6 5 4 3 2 1

To Barbara, with fond memories
of "the Chatterboxes"

One

Jake Mallory scrawled his signature on the hotel registration card before he could change his mind and head for the nearest exit.

As he pushed the completed card across the counter, he glanced around the lobby. The Somerset Inn's blend of informality and elegance appealed to him. If the rooms were equally pleasant, the small hotel would be perfect for an extended stay. He suspected, however, that he'd be checking out first thing in the morning. Unless . . .

"Here you are, Mr. Mallory." The desk clerk held out his room key. "Third floor, turn right when you get off the elevator. I'll have your bags sent up pronto, and if there's anything you need, just call. My name's Trudy."

"Thanks, Trudy," Jake said with a quick smile. Taking the key and slipping it into his jacket pocket, he asked carefully, "Is Brittany Thomas in? She's the manager here, isn't she?"

"Britt's on her lunch break right now," Trudy answered, then checked the overhead clock behind her. "But she should be back in about ten minutes."

Ten minutes. The innocuous phrase made Jake's heart leap and his pulse race crazily. Just ten more minutes. "Would you take a message for her, Trudy?" he asked, annoyed by the sudden tightness in his voice. He'd vowed to stay cool.

Pencil and memo pad at the ready, the clerk looked up at him.

Jake smiled. "Not that kind of message, Trudy." He bent down to pick up the narrow plastic bag he'd left on the floor beside his briefcase, took out a single long-stemmed peach rose and a card, and placed them on the counter. "This kind."

A slight arching of one brow betrayed Trudy's curiosity. "Would you like Britt to call you in your suite as soon as she gets back?"

"No, I'll wait for her," Jake said firmly. He wanted to see Brittany's honest reaction, not a prepared response. Glancing toward a vacant wing chair in the sitting area to his left, he added, "Right over there."

He headed for the chair, sat down, picked up a newspaper from a nearby table, and tried to read while the long minutes ticked by.

As she strode across the lobby of the Somerset after her lunchtime walk in the park, Brittany's thoughts were so far away that she didn't spy the rose until she went up to the front desk to collect her mail.

Her heartbeat skidded to a stop, and she felt the blood drain from her face. It was a coincidence, she told herself. Lots of people liked long-stemmed peach roses.

She saw the card with her name on it just as Trudy

picked up the rose and handed it to her. "For you," the clerk said, beaming. "Did you ever see anything so perfect?"

"Once," Brittany murmured, tracing the edges of the outer petals with her fingertip as if to make sure they were real.

"Aren't you going to open the card?" Trudy urged with an expectant smile.

Brittany took the envelope, willing herself to use careful, methodical movements. But she shook out the card with trembling hands, and as she read it, her legs almost buckled under her. The message was short and to the point: *Kitten: Dinner this evening?*

Kitten.

The blood returned to Brittany's cheeks in a rush of erotic heat as she remembered how she'd inspired that nickname. "It can't be," she whispered, then snapped out of her trance and looked questioningly at Trudy. "Where did this come from?"

"A guest who just checked in," Trudy answered, no longer smiling. "Are you okay, Britt?"

"I'm fine," Brittany answered, though her quavering voice belied her words. As she slipped the card into her blazer pocket, her heart was pounding so hard, it echoed in her ears. "This . . . guest. Do you know where he is now?"

"I put him in three-oh-six, but he's not there," Trudy said, then looked toward the sitting area. "He's right over—"

"Jake," Brittany said, very softly, following Trudy's glance. Suddenly her world was tilting so sharply on its axis, she found herself clutching onto the edge of the counter for dear life.

Jake Mallory was folding a newspaper and getting to his feet, his smoky gray gaze locked on hers, his heavy brows lifting at the inner corners like two sides of a half-raised drawbridge. His quizzical expression—the very one that had been haunting her dreams and most of her waking hours for six months—twisted Brittany's insides into a knot of raw yearning.

Forcing herself to move toward Jake with an outward show of poise, Brittany felt as if she were trying to negotiate a moving sidewalk that had run amok.

As she slowly emerged from her shock, she noticed that he had lost weight. Although he still looked like a Titan who'd escaped from some Greek legend into the real world of smaller men and lesser deeds, he was thinner than Brittany remembered. His beige slacks, yellow polo shirt, and tan leather jacket hung loosely on his body, and his craggy features had become even sharper. He didn't look as if he'd been ill exactly, but something had deepened the vertical creases bracketing his mouth. Something had added new, harder lines to the appealing crinkles at the corners of his eyes.

Brittany assumed the change was the result of exposure to the tropical sun, until she realized that Jake's bronze glow had faded, not intensified, and his ash-brown hair was shot with fewer gold streaks.

What had happened to Jake since she'd seen him last?

Brittany stopped and gave her head a shake. Never mind what had happened to Jake, what was happening to *her*? One look at Jake Mallory and she was bewitched.

She had to pull herself together. She had to say something. "Jake," she murmured again, then stopped. Her throat had closed over.

He gazed at her in silence for several charged moments. Finally he spoke, his voice as rough as an uncut diamond. "Hello, Brittany. It's been a long time."

"You remembered," she said in a husky whisper, still clutching the long stem of the peach rose. "The rose is the same color."

Her remark brought a tiny smile to his lips. "Of course I remembered."

Brittany nodded, but she was at a loss to understand what Jake was doing at the Somerset. Was she dreaming this whole scene? "I don't suppose this is a coincidence, is it? Your staying here, I mean?"

"No, it isn't," Jake answered. "It isn't even a coincidence that I'm in Vancouver, Brittany. And I'm not here as a consulting engineer on some construction site. I've come to see you. To find out why—"

"This isn't a good place to talk," Brittany cut in with an anxious glance around the lobby.

Jake refused to be put off. "Then where? Over dinner tonight?"

"I . . . I don't think dinner would be a good idea," Brittany forced herself to say, though she wanted desperately to accept.

"Brittany, we're going to talk," Jake said quietly. "You're going to tell me what went wrong. Maybe I'm being presumptuous, but I think you owe me that much."

Searching his eyes, she saw unfamiliar shards of flint embedded in the velvety gray depths. "I do owe you that much," she conceded with a sigh. "You're not being presumptuous."

"How about your office?" Jake suggested. "Right now, or later this afternoon—you name the time and place."

"My office wouldn't work." Brittany managed a quick, nervous smile. "It's Grand Central in there."

"My suite, then?"

Her knees almost gave out. The two of them, alone in his hotel suite. Dear heaven, she couldn't have backed herself into a more explosive situation. Memories were flooding her already, engulfing her in a warm rush of desire and eroding the fragile handhold of common sense she was clinging to. But she hadn't left herself much leeway. And after all, Jake was a gentleman. She could trust him—even if she couldn't trust herself.

"Brittany?" he prompted, his voice gentle.

She swallowed hard and nodded. "In about half an hour?" she ventured, hoping to buy some time to calm down. "Or would you prefer to unpack and get settled first?" she added eagerly.

Jake gave her a crooked smile. "I think we'd better talk before I unpack."

So much for buying time, Brittany thought. Well, maybe the best thing would be to get this confrontation over with. "Should we make it a quarter of an hour?"

"Sounds perfect," Jake answered.

"It does?" Brittany said in a small voice, then hastily pulled herself together. "I mean . . . fine. Good. Room three-oh-six in fifteen minutes." Turning on her heel, she retreated across the lobby toward the temporary haven of her office, feeling Jake's intense gaze following her until she was out of sight.

Brittany's three quick raps on Jake's door precisely fifteen minutes after she'd left him sounded like a summons to a kangaroo court. But Brittany was the defendant, Jake reminded himself. He wasn't going to let her take over as prosecutor, judge, and jury.

He hesitated before going to the door, taking a deep breath and tightening his stomach muscles as if bracing for a blow to the solar plexus. What if she'd broken her promise to keep in touch because she'd found someone else? Jake had convinced himself he was ready to hear that explanation for her months of silence, but all at once he wasn't certain. Her reaction to his rose—and to him—had stirred his hopes.

Just seeing her again had shaken him more than he'd thought it would, confirming what hadn't needed confirmation: Brittany Thomas still got to him in a way no other woman ever had in all his thirty-seven years. Strange, he thought, at last heading toward the door. Brittany wasn't his type. He'd always been drawn to sleek, pampered, exotic types. He liked tall, willowy women. Women with raven or platinum or flaming-red hair. Women who wore expensive clothes and favored subtle neutrals or stark, dramatic black. Women who moved as if the world would wait for them and whose all-knowing eyes tossed out a challenge to a predatory male.

But Brittany? That curvaceous imp with unruly chestnut hair, a ready grin, and a taste for the colors of a riotous garden? That dynamo who approached life as if it were an apple tree laden with ripe fruit that she intended to shake down?

Reaching the door, he threw it open and grinned broadly, just as he had when he'd first seen Brittany burst into the hotel lobby earlier. In her hot pink blazer and a silk dress that seemed to have been inspired by a Gauguin painting, she was a tonic for his tired spirits.

Jake's smile faded as he looked into Brittany's luminous brown eyes. She hadn't knocked on his door peremptorily, he realized. She'd bounced her knuckles off it with the bravado of a trick-or-treating kid facing down the neighborhood grouch on a dare. And she was ready to bolt if he said, "Boo." "Hi," he said instead, trying to sound nonthreatening. "You're very prompt."

She shot him a smile so fleeting and minuscule, he wondered if he'd imagined it. Then, by turning sideways as she entered, she ensured there'd be no contact between their bodies.

Jake chose to interpret her physical wariness as a victory for him. Apparently she hadn't forgotten the conflagration that ignited whenever they touched. He watched in bemused silence as she stalked into his living room to the farthest wall, then looked around as if for an escape hatch. Jake was glad there wasn't one.

He closed the door and went to the minifridge in one corner of the room. "There seems to be an ample supply of everything from diet soda to liqueurs here," he said, determined to give himself the advantage by being calm. "Can I offer you a drink?"

"No, thank you," Brittany said politely, pacing back and forth in front of the wide window that offered a panoramic view of English Bay. "I can't stay long."

"I see," Jake murmured.

Brittany stopped, her back to Jake as she stared out at the silver-blue Pacific, her hands grasping the windowsill as if it were the railing of a storm-tossed ship. "What did you mean by that comment you made downstairs?" she asked after a deep, shaky breath.

Jake frowned. "What comment?"

"You said you wouldn't unpack until we've talked. Are you suggesting you'll leave the Somerset unless

I . . . well . . . encourage you to stay? Was it some kind of ultimatum?"

"Hardly," he answered, taken aback by her total misinterpretation of his intent. "I was trying to be considerate, Brittany. I'd hate to create an awkward situation for both of us by staying here at the Somerset, that's all."

She finally turned to face him, thrusting splayed fingers through her hair to push back a wayward cowlick. "I'm sorry," she said in a low voice, then shook her head and laughed softly. "I think I've spent the past fifteen minutes reaching for any excuse I can find to be testy with you," she admitted reluctantly. Her gaze darted everywhere in the room but at Jake.

"Brittany, try to look at me when we're talking, will you?" Jake said gently.

Very slowly, steeling herself to withstand his impact, Brittany obeyed. But as Jake filled her entire field of vision, her emotional armor dissolved. He'd taken off his jacket, and even though he was leaner than he'd been six months earlier, he was no less magnificent. The sight of his muscular arms made Brittany ache to feel them around her. His mouth brought back a rush of phantom kisses that made her lips tingle as if he'd possessed them only moments before, and her hands itched to explore every hard, taut inch of him. "Jake," she whispered, almost to herself. "Jake, what am I doing here? Am I out of my mind? Why would I walk into a room knowing I'd be alone with you?"

Jake's lips curved in a slow, sensuous smile as he began moving toward her. "You do feel something for me," he said with a note of surprise in his deep voice. "At the very least you want me. You want me as much as I want you."

Both Brittany's hands shot up, palms forward, as if to ward him off. "Don't come any closer. *Please* don't!"

"Why?" Jake asked, though he stopped and assumed a relaxed stance, feet astride and hands resting loosely on hips.

Brittany swallowed hard. Jake's every gesture underscored his uncompromising masculinity, as unnerving as it was fascinating. "Because . . . because wanting isn't enough," she forced herself to answer, trying to persuade herself more than Jake.

"Wanting is a pretty good start," he countered.

Lowering her hands, Brittany folded her arms across her midriff. "A start to what?"

"I'm not sure," Jake said gently. "But I'd like to find out. Wouldn't you?"

She shook her head. "Not when I know where things would end."

"Then you know more than I do, Brittany." Jake paused, studying her, then asked the hateful but necessary question. "Is there someone else?"

"Of course not," she shot back without a second's hesitation, as if he'd just made the most ridiculous suggestion she'd ever heard. And it did seem ludicrous to her. Jake had witnessed her reaction to the romantic token he'd left for her at the front desk. How could he imagine she would respond that way if she were involved with another man? "Just because the last time we were together, I acted . . . impulsively," she said, then stopped, wondering why she was being so euphemistic. Why not call a spade a spade? "Just because I slept with you the night we met doesn't mean I go around collecting males and putting notches on my headboard," she said with a defiant lift of her chin.

Jake's eyes narrowed to iron-gray slits. "Slept with me?"

"You know what I mean," Brittany mumbled, her attempt at worldliness instantly fizzling. She turned again toward the window.

Someone down on Sunset Beach was putting a trio of colorful kites through a graceful sky ballet, and Brittany watched with exaggerated attention, pretending not to be aware of Jake's gaze boring a hole in her back.

When she'd braved the lion's den by coming to Jake's room, she'd underestimated—or forgotten—how he dominated his surroundings with the sheer force of his presence. The hotel suite itself seemed to have adapted to his requirements, though Brittany knew this was because of Trudy's peculiar talent for matching people to rooms. This one, with its generously proportioned furnishings and restful earth tones, happened to be right for Jake.

But there was no denying that Jake Mallory was a man who staked out a territory and made it his own, even if his possession was to be temporary.

What worried Brittany was the possibility that she was earmarked as part of that territory. A temporary possession.

She sensed rather than heard a movement behind her. Feeling the heat of Jake's body no more than an inch from hers, she stiffened, battling the instinct to lean back against him as he curved his hands around her shoulders and bent to brush his lips over her temple.

"My recollection of that night in San Francisco must be somewhat more romantic than yours," he murmured against her ear, his warm breath caressing her skin and sending shivers through her whole body.

"Jake, don't do this to me," she pleaded with a catch in her voice.

He went on as if he hadn't heard her. "I remember how we kept crossing each other's paths all day at the hotel, making eye contact and smiling, pretending not to notice the instant sparks between us."

"You picked me up," Brittany said raggedly. "That's what it was, you know. I let you pick me up, and I don't *do* that sort of thing."

Jake reached up with both hands and slid his fingers under her shoulder-length hair, lifting and moving it to one side so that he could touch his lips to the nape of her neck. "Don't cheapen what we shared, Brittany. I saw you sitting alone in the dining room and knew I couldn't let the chance to know you slip by, so I sent the rose and the note with the waiter asking you to have dinner with me." Trailing kisses upward to the sensitive skin behind her ear, he went on with gentle persuasion. "I wasn't surprised when you started shaking your head no even before you'd finished reading the note. I knew I was going for a long shot, and you were likely to turn me down. But then you glanced up and saw me." As he spoke, Jake blazed a path of searing kisses down the side of Brittany's throat. "I'll never forget the smile that lit up your face, or the surprise in your eyes when you found yourself nodding after all."

Brittany couldn't forget either. It had been the strangest sensation to look into Jake's eyes and feel herself succumbing to the temptation he offered. "I couldn't say no to you," she confessed, her voice becoming thick with desire. "Not at that moment, and not later . . . when, heaven help me, I should have."

"Sweetheart, our lovemaking that night was natural and inevitable. Don't ever look back on it with regret. It was beautiful, and special . . . and haunting."

Haunting, Brittany repeated silently. She closed her eyes, wondering how many times during the past six months she'd relived those hours, remembering how perfectly attuned she and Jake had been. Whether talking over dinner, dancing to old ballads afterward, or making love until dawn, they'd seemed so right together.

Yet the whole thing had been so wrong, she reminded herself, biting down on her lower lip to stifle a moan. She'd been in San Francisco for a weekend convention. Jake was passing through on his way to Australia, just one more stop in his rolling-stone existence. If their brief encounter had been inevitable, their separation the next morning had been even more so. She'd boarded her northbound plane to Vancouver. Jake had seen her off before going through his gate. She remembered feeling as if she were saying good-bye to an essential part of herself.

Only after she'd been away from Jake and his spellbinding magic for a few hours had she been appalled by what she'd done. She realized that Jake was a man to dream about, not to get involved with. By his own admission he'd been a nomad all his life, emotionally as well as geographically.

It had been impossible to forget Jake, but time and distance had returned her to a modicum of reason she was trying to hold on to now. It was her only defense against the insane compulsion to surrender to him again. She was dizzy with wanting him, aching with an inner emptiness only he could fill.

"Don't you understand?" she cried softly, negating her protests with a helpless arching of her throat that invited more of his tantalizing kisses. "I'm not myself when I'm with you. All my rules are suspended. My common sense goes out the window, and my will is nonexistent."

"By a strange coincidence you make me feel exactly the same way," he said huskily, sliding his arms around her waist. Pressed against the hard length of his body, she could be in no doubt of her effect on him.

Brittany desperately twisted around to face him, flattening her palms against his chest with every intention of pushing him away. But his arms enfolded her with a strength and tenderness she couldn't fight, and when she felt his heart beating with erratic violence, she looked up at him in surprise. He seemed so invincible, yet his accelerated heartbeat said he wasn't.

"Brittany," Jake murmured, his eyes dark with a tumult of emotion, "I've imagined you so often, I'm finding it difficult to believe you're real." *Difficult*? he thought. *More like impossible.* The events of the past few months had rearranged his priorities. The plan to talk to Brittany at least once more had become paramount—second only to actual survival. He'd told himself he only wanted to be certain he had no chance with her so that he could put her out of his mind and get on with his life. Even when he'd arrived at the Somerset, he'd believed his self-deception.

Now that she was in his arms, he knew better. He wasn't sure anymore what his plan was, but he was certain he didn't want to let her go. Not without a fight. And now that he knew the best weapon in his arsenal, he would use it mercilessly.

Brittany saw the intent in Jake's eyes. "Don't do this to me," she whispered again.

When he lowered his mouth to hers, his kiss was as gentle and sweet as a wintergreen-scented breeze. "Whatever I'm doing to you, sweetheart, you're doing to me as well," he murmured against her lips, then stroked them with the tip of his tongue until they parted for him.

Brittany's arms crept around Jake's neck, and her fingers began sifting through the thick, silky hair that reached almost to his collar. Her body grew pliant, melting against his, her curves and hollows effortlessly fitting themselves to his rigid planes. She lost track of time and place as his kiss deepened. If he'd lifted her in his arms and carried her to his bedroom, she'd have made no protest.

But Jake's grip on sanity was apparently stronger than hers. He raised his head and gazed down at her, the strain of controlling himself evident in the hard set of his features. "If I make love to you now, Brittany, you'll run scared afterward. You'll torment yourself—and me—with more regrets. And I'll do the same, because I've waited too long to settle for a moment stolen from your workday."

"Workday?" Brittany repeated in a small voice, then blinked and let out a groan of dismay. "Oh, Lord, I'm supposed to be running this hotel, not . . . not . . . What's the *matter* with me?"

"Not a thing, as far as I can tell," Jake said with a smile.

Brittany tried to wrench herself out of his arms, but she couldn't move. "Aren't you going to let me go?" she asked with a surprised frown. Jake was a forceful male, but not pushy.

"Maybe I will, maybe not," he teased. A playful glint appeared in his eyes. "Maybe I'll keep you here after all, until I've heard your contented purr."

He could do anything he liked with her, Brittany thought helplessly. A little of his tender persuasion was all it took. That was what frightened her.

Suddenly Jake gave a low chuckle. "Don't look so

alarmed, Brittany. I'm prepared to let you go—if you'll agree to have dinner with me tonight." When she opened her mouth to protest, he planted a quick kiss on her lips. "If you'll give me that much, I promise not to let you end the evening by luring me into the nearest bed. I'll be strong. I'll resist you."

Brittany tried to glare at him, but couldn't keep the amused gleam out of her eyes. "Such humility," she drawled.

"And I'll listen attentively if you want to explain the insurmountable obstacles you see between us," Jake went on, ignoring her irony.

Lifting both brows, she said, "You mean you *need* an explanation? You know perfectly well our lives are on separate tracks, Jake. They converged for that one lovely night, but they went off again in different directions, and that's the way it'll always be. I'm a nest builder, and you're a—"

"Save all that fine logic for tonight," Jake interrupted. "That is, unless you want to go back to Plan A."

Brittany tilted her head to one side and studied him with sudden wariness. "What's Plan A?" she asked, though she suspected she already knew.

Jake's arms tightened like a vise as he looked down at her with a roguish grin. "I keep you here now and make love to you until you're ready to listen to reason."

"You wouldn't," Brittany replied without much conviction. Her pulse rocketed as she watched Jake's expression lose its playfulness, his eyes turning to anthracite and focusing on her mouth. She was dealing with an unpredictable male whose sensual power over her was irresistible. "Dinner tonight will be fine," she said in a small voice.

For a breathless moment Jake didn't react, as if

he'd decided she hadn't answered quickly enough. But at last he nodded, kissed the tip of her nose, and released her. "I'll pick you up at seven."

"Seven-thirty," Brittany amended, simply to make the point that she wouldn't be dictated to. Heading for the door, she was surprised her trembling legs would carry her.

"Your address?" Jake asked, following her. "You moved after that night in San Francisco."

Brittany told him, then paused as she reached for the doorknob. "Jake, what is it you really want from me?"

He gazed at her for another long moment before finally answering. "I have no idea, Brittany. I only know what I *don't* want."

"Which is?"

"To let you go a second time," he said softly.

As her heart leapt into her throat, Brittany pulled open the door and bolted.

Two

Brittany closed her office door and leaned against it, her thoughts whirling.

She couldn't *believe* she'd agreed to have dinner with Jake! Hadn't she paced this very office just a little while earlier, rehearsing at least half a dozen ways to tell him she wouldn't pick up where they'd left off? Why had she given in? It wasn't as if she really believed he'd have used his unique brand of persuasion.

Or did she?

It occurred to her that she didn't know Jake at all. She'd been more intimate with him than she'd ever dreamed possible, yet he was almost a stranger to her. Just how far *would* he go to get what he wanted? And why was he so adamant about wanting her? He must have his choice of far more sophisticated women all over the world. Why was he going out of his way to pursue someone who obviously wasn't in his league? Was it simply the conquest he enjoyed? Did she rate a special effort because she happened to be the one that got away?

With a deep sigh Brittany went to her desk to force herself to get back to her duties as manager of the Somerset, telling herself that going out with Jake might not be such a bad idea after all. He'd said he would listen to her arguments over dinner. Fine. She would be able to deliver her speech in a setting public enough to keep her from succumbing to his magic again.

The remainder of Brittany's afternoon was a total loss. She couldn't concentrate on routine matters, and not one thorny problem arose to absorb her attention.

What was worse, her agitation seemed to be obvious, at least to her boss. During an afternoon chat in the coffee shop, Helena Danforth, who owned the Somerset and had lived in one of its penthouse apartments since her husband's death five years before, asked Brittany whether their temperamental chef had been throwing tantrums and upsetting her.

"Not at all," Brittany said with a smile. "I find I enjoy the challenge of settling Sandro down after one of his rages. But he's been quiet for a couple of days." She laughed. "Maybe too quiet."

Helena patted her short white hair and lifted her shoulders in a casual little shrug, but her blue eyes brightened with curiosity. "Well, if it isn't Sandro, something else has you wandering around in the clouds, young lady."

"Why do you say that?" Brittany asked, taken aback by Helena's perceptiveness.

"Oh, I don't know," Helena drawled, her quiet voice laced with amusement. "Perhaps it's because I just mentioned that my friend the police chief told me there's been a rash of hotel break-ins in the neighborhood, and you said that was nice."

Blushing furiously, Brittany stiffened her resolve

to get Jake Mallory out of her life. She launched into an impromptu list of extra precautions that could be taken against burglars and tried to ignore Helena's knowing smile.

When Chef Sandro sent up a message asking Brittany to see him in the kitchen around four-thirty, she noted wryly her eager response to his summons. Jake really was bending her mind if she was starting to hope for a full-fledged Sandro crisis. Preferably one that would give her an excuse to cancel dinner.

All the chef wanted, however, was to give Brittany some custard he'd made for her best friend, Casey McLean. "To stop the heartfire from the *bambino*," he explained.

"Heartfire?" she repeated blankly, too distracted to be as quick as usual to translate the chef's fractured idioms. "Heartfire from the *bambino*?"

Sandro rolled his eyes and laughed. "Whatsa matter, *bella*, you don't understand English? Heartfire!" He touched his stomach, crossed his eyes, and lolled out his tongue in clarification.

Brittany nodded, thanked Sandro effusively, and told him she was certain the custard would ease the heartburn of Casey's pregnancy.

"Maybe you eat some too," he suggested. "You no look so good, *bella*. You have a fever maybe?"

Brittany laughed nervously, said she was fine, and hurried back to her office to peer at herself in the mirror. Sandro was right, she acknowledged. She did have a fever: Jake Mallory Fever.

She decided to book off early to deliver the treat to Casey before going home to get dressed for dinner. Apparently nothing was going to get her out of it.

Tingling with a mixture of anticipation and dread, Brittany sped along the streets of Vancouver's West

End toward the offices of the *Weekender*, the neighborhood newspaper Casey and her husband, Alex, owned.

Casey wasn't at the *Weekender*. She'd taken the afternoon off to do some work at home, one of the typesetters told Brittany.

Amazing, Brittany thought as she hurried to the run-down mansion the McLeans were restoring to its former elegance. *Casey, the original workaholic journalist, was turning so domestic, she would take an afternoon off? Love did seem to have a way of transforming people.*

Love, maybe. But infatuation? Raw desire? Longings that made no sense and just led to eventual pain?

Brittany found Casey, her strawberry-blond hair in a haphazard topknot of curls and wearing her most comfortable grubs, perched on a stepladder attacking the layers of wallpaper in one of the back rooms of the charming old house.

Brittany put down the box containing the bowl of custard. "Sandro sent you a treat, Casey. He says it will help you eat in spite of your morning sickness. Does your husband know you're doing so much physical work around here? Didn't he say he wanted to hire people for this sort of thing?"

"Alex is overprotective," Casey answered blithely, hopping down from the ladder. She opened the box and beamed when she peered inside. "Sandro's such a sweetheart. He knows his custard is one of the few things I can enjoy these days."

"You're still feeling rotten?"

"Mostly just fed up. Why do they call it morning sickness, anyhow? How about morning-noon-and-night sickness?" Casey said good-naturedly, then frowned as she looked more closely at Brittany. "But what's with you, Britt? You look awfully flushed, and your eyes have a funny glaze. . . ."

"I've been rushing," Brittany cut in hastily, deciding she either had to learn to mask her emotions or start associating with less observant people. "And I'd better keep moving," she went on. "There are rain clouds gathering, and I don't have my umbrella."

Casey invited her to stay for a bite to eat, but Brittany mumbled a vague excuse about dashing off to a dinner meeting.

As she raced homeward, she wondered why she'd never confided in Casey about Jake. At the time she'd met him, she'd been too shattered to talk about the experience with anyone, even her best friend. But now . . .

Now there was no point mentioning him. By the end of the evening Jake would be history—if she had to resort to hair curlers, face cream, and a wilted flannel robe to make him back off.

Watching Brittany stride across her apartment building's lobby, Jake took in the dazzle of her bright turquoise raincoat and a flash of the coral silk dress under it. Her hair, cascading in soft waves to her shoulders, glinted with strands of gold, and her lips were as inviting as a ripe nectarine.

She looked special, he mused, a smile tugging at the corners of his mouth. *She looked like a woman who'd put a lot of effort into dressing to please a man.*

She still carried herself, however, more like a jungle cat than a cuddly kitten, as if she was determined to deny the softer side of her nature. Jake was intrigued by her feistiness. It was part of what excited him.

Realizing that his male instincts had gone on red alert and his blood was catching fire like a trail of gasoline touched by an open flame, Jake reminded himself that he'd made Brittany a promise. Their evening wouldn't end in bed.

He took a deep breath to steady himself, but Brittany drew near just at that moment, and he inhaled her intoxicating scent. *Sweetheart*, he silently told her, *if you hope to convince me to make a quiet retreat from your life, you're going about it the wrong way.*

He took her hand, tucked it under his arm, and gave it a little squeeze against his body. "You probably know this," he said with a warmth he couldn't hide, "but I'll tell you anyway: Miss Thomas, you look terrific."

Brittany tried to meet his smoldering gaze with a cool smile, but she had to look away or risk melting into a coral-and-turquoise puddle. "You're something of a traffic stopper yourself, Mr. Mallory," she managed to say with only a slight catch in her voice. In his open beige raincoat, camel blazer, dark brown slacks, and a lightweight white sweater, Jake exuded virility and his own brand of offhand masculine glamour.

A stream of unbidden memories flooded Brittany's imagination and caught her up in a dizzying flow of sensuality. Jake, the first time she'd seen him, mysterious and elegant in a sleekly tailored dark suit, his white dress shirt gleaming against the bronze of his skin. Jake, his jacket and tie off and his shirtsleeves rolled up as he offered her a snifter of cognac in his suite, his fingers brushing against hers and his gray eyes hypnotic. Jake, gloriously naked, moving toward her as she waited in his bed. . . .

"My car's right outside, and there isn't much rain

at the moment," he said as he pushed open one of the double glass doors of the building's main entrance.

Brittany stared up at him, disoriented. Car? Rain?

"I didn't think we'd need an umbrella," Jake explained when he saw her lost expression.

Brittany nodded and smiled, but wondered how on earth she expected to turn Jake off when he had such a devastating way of turning her *on*.

Jake drove into the hills of North Vancouver to a small Japanese restaurant that was new to Brittany, complete with shoji screens, seductively gentle koto music in the background, gracious waitresses dressed in traditional geisha costumes, and embroidered silk slippers to replace the shoes they'd left at the entrance to their small, private dining room.

Brittany swallowed hard as she surveyed the intimate setting. So much for delivering her speech in a public place, she thought with a frisson of reluctant excitement.

"Vancouver's supposed to be my town, not yours." she commented brightly when they were settled on cushions at the low table. "And I'm in the hospitality business here. How would you know about a place I've never heard of?"

Jake smiled, pleased to have surprised her. "Anybody who travels as much as I do learns to zero in on great little off-the-beaten-track restaurants. And over the years I've spent a fair amount of time in Vancouver. It's not all that far from California, so I've worked on quite a few assignments here."

"You've been based in California for some time, haven't you?" Brittany said with studied casualness. A little small talk before the heavy conversation seemed in order, given the serenity of their surroundings.

"I've kept an office and a small apartment in Santa Barbara for the past ten years, though I haven't spent much time there," Jake answered as he picked up the slender porcelain container of warmed sake the waitress had delivered. "My engineering contracts keep me on the move, usually in remote corners of the world. . . ." He shot Brittany a bland smile. "As you're probably aware."

"I trust you have someone to water your plants," Brittany said, then wished she could bit her tongue. Her banter sounded suspiciously like a fishing expedition.

Jake laughed quietly. "I don't have plants. They can tie a person down almost as much as pets."

Or children, Brittany added silently. *Or . . .*

"I do have a woman keeping an eye on things at the apartment," Jake went on.

I'll just bet you do, Brittany thought, but flashed him an unconcerned smile.

Jake looked quizzically at her, as if not sure what she was smiling about. "And another who runs my office as efficiently as if it were her own," he added.

"How nice to have people you can count on," Brittany said pleasantly.

After filling two tiny matching cups with sake, Jake passed one to Brittany and raised the other in a salute. *"Kanpai,"* he said with a smile.

She hesitated, then brightened and said, *"Sayonara."*

His heavy brows quirked upward, and his cup remained suspended halfway to his mouth. "Goodbye? Again?"

Exactly, Brittany thought. But she didn't say it. It was the second time she'd missed a perfect chance to get to the point of the evening. "It's the only Japanese word I know," she confessed.

"Then allow me to teach you some others," Jake urged. "'Hello,' for starters." He turned on the full heat of his gaze as he let it sweep slowly over her. "Or better still, let's concentrate on words like—"

"You speak Japanese?" Brittany broke in, suspecting what kinds of words he had in mind. Her whole body was responding to his visual caress, from her irregular breathing to her heightened color. "You've actually learned the language?"

"Enough to get by," Jake answered. "I tend to pick up my vocabulary from the people I meet rather than by studying formally, so I suspect there are some odd idiosyncrascies in my speech." Though his comment was modest enough, his eyes were agleam as he raised his sake cup to his lips.

Realizing that Jake was enjoying his power to arouse her with a mere look, Brittany feigned innocence and determindedly stuck to small talk. "How many languages do you know, anyway?"

"A couple, if you're talking about a certain level of mastery. Otherwise, smatterings of several and a passing acquaintance with some obscure tribal tongues in the South Pacific and Africa." Jake shrugged. He seemed to have very little interest in boasting about his accomplishments. "As I said, enough to get by."

Perhaps Jake wasn't being modest, Brittany thought. Perhaps he didn't know more than "enough to get by" in several languages. Maybe he carried his pocket *Swahili Made Easy* or whatever, and otherwise managed to make his meaning clear with gestures. He was a past master at silent communication, and after all, how long could it take to learn a few sweep-them-off-their-feet phrases?

Suddenly she knew she was up to her old tricks again, searching for some reason to be antagonistic toward Jake. *Cheap tactic,* she chided herself. Jake's charm wasn't a character flaw, even if it was convenient for her to think so. Why not enjoy the man while she could?

Dishes arrived at their table, obviously preordered: a clear broth sprinkled with fresh herbs, a salad that looked like a miniature bouquet while teasing the taste buds with its ginger-laced dressing, and platters offering generous samplings of succulent tempura shrimp and vegetables as well as teriyaki chicken and beef.

Jake was a smooth and gracious host, and Brittany felt herself not only enjoying him but slipping under his spell, no matter how she fought his drugging effect. He managed to find the chink in her armor without seeming to try. She'd steeled herself against his untrammeled masculinity. She could cope with the sensual sparks he ignited inside her. But what she hadn't been ready for was the about-face in Jake's manner. Except for the initial moments of mild flirtation, he became so proper—almost impersonal—that Brittany began wondering if something she'd said or done had dampened his desire for her. The way he was acting, it was as if she'd told Casey the truth—as if she really were having a business dinner.

"There've been a few changes in your life in the past six months," Jake said after complimenting Brittany on her mastery of chopsticks. "When we met, you were sales director at the Pacific Inn. Now you're a manager at the Somerset."

"It's a much smaller hotel," Brittany pointed out.

"But a no less luxurious one," Jake countered.

"How did you land such a prestigious job when you hadn't been even an assistant manager before?"

"Sheer luck, mainly. I was in the right place at the right time and had met Helena Danforth a couple of months before she started looking for a new manager." Rattled by the subtle change in Jake, Brittany chattered on more freely than normal, filling him in on details he had no reason to be interested in. She told him that Helena owned the Somerset but had needed someone to run it for her ever since her husband's death. "Danforth Developments is a big real estate and construction firm that takes up most of Helena's time," Brittany explained. "But she didn't want to sell the hotel because it's always been *her* baby, not part of the larger company."

"Given the risks in the construction business, I imagine her husband wanted it that way," Jake commented.

"He did, as a matter of fact," Brittany said, raising her eyebrows. Most people seemed surprised to learn that the Somerset had been kept as a separate entity, not understanding that David Danforth had insisted on protecting the hotel against any reverses in his heavily leveraged ventures. Obviously Jake and David Danforth thought along the same lines.

Making parallels between Jake and David Danforth didn't do much for Brittany's peace of mind. Everything she'd heard about Helena's late husband made him seem like a romance hero—powerful and aggressive, yet caring, considerate, and genuinely respectful of his wife's abilities.

Clearing her throat, Brittany went on with even more agitation, "Helena had an excellent manager for the Somerset who apparently seemed content to run the place forever, but about a year ago he went to a bigger hotel. Helena tried to stay on top of things for a few months, but the load was too heavy for anyone, let alone a woman in her midsixties who'd never planned to be a high-powered executive in the first place. I happened along, expecting Helena to commend my enthusiasm and tell me to go back and pile up a little more experience. Instead she decided to take a chance on me. So far I seem to be doing all right. Helena's a wonderful boss—a mentor actually. And a friend."

"I'm sure she knows she's lucky to have you," Jake commented, smiling at Brittany in a way that suddenly reassured her his feelings toward her were anything but impersonal.

Suffused by a rush of warmth that coursed through every part of her being, Brittany had to give herself a hard mental shake to remind herself that she was supposed to *want* Jake to be impersonal. "How was Australia?" she asked in an unnaturally bright tone, deciding it was time to focus the attention on him.

"Australia was fine when I left it four months ago," Jake answered, refilling their sake cups.

Although she was aware of his implied rebuke for her unnecessary ignorance of his travels during the past four months, Brittany chose to pretend she hadn't read between the lines. "And after Australia?" she prompted. "What was your next stop?"

Instead of answering, Jake toyed with the food on his plate, pushing it from side to side with the chopsticks.

"Top secret?" Brittany said lightly.

He looked up and flashed her a smile that seemed more forced than real. "No, just boring. I'd rather listen to you tell me more about your job at the Somerset."

Brittany went along with his sidestep, but while

she was speaking enthusiastically again about her job and Helena and all the denizens of the Somerset, she was wondering what kind of secrets Jake preferred not to share with her.

Undoubtedly they had something to do with a woman, she decided unhappily. She'd been in the hotel business long enough to know that when a traveling male became evasive, there was usually a woman lurking in the background—or several women, none of whom knew about one another. She doubted whether Jake was being discreetly quiet about his devoted assistant and his apartment-sitter in Santa Barbara. More likely he was brooding about someone he'd met wherever his last assignment had taken him—someone mysterious and gorgeous who could cast her own spells and weave her own magic, someone whose impact on a man could shake him enough to send him back to a vulnerable rube in Vancouver for an ego boost.

Abruptly Brittany decided to say her piece. Dinner was almost over, and they could leave as soon as she'd made Jake understand she had no intention of becoming a charter member of his global harem.

As if sensing what she was about to do, Jake suddenly began talking about his travels—those he chose to discuss, at any rate. He sketched a quick autobiography, from his military-brat upbringing to his adventures as a free-lance engineer, living for brief periods in places most people had never heard of. His anecdotes were funny and fascinating, and Brittany was captivated against her will. He was like a male Scheherazade, spinning stories that mesmerized her.

They had left the restaurant and were almost back at her place before the magic began to dissipate as she realized she *still* hadn't told Jake that she wasn't going to have an affair with him, no matter how susceptible she appeared to be.

Not sure why she'd put off the inevitable moment of truth, Brittany blamed Jake. He was clearly a master manipulator—another reason to keep her distance and further evidence that she wasn't in his league.

When they reached her building, Jake insisted on seeing her right to her door. His hand, placed lightly on the small of her back, radiated heat throughout her body, but she stiffened her spine and told herself to be strong.

Her movements were jerky as she opened her purse to dig out her apartment key. When she tried in vain to fit it into the lock, she swore under her breath at her clumsiness.

Jake closed his hand over hers, took the key, and calmly unlocked the door.

Brittany felt like throttling him for being so unruffled, but she turned to say a polite good night. It was too late for her stupid speech anyway. Maybe he'd get the hint or grow bored and simply leave town.

But Jake suddenly whisked her inside her apartment, shut the door behind them, and took her in his arms. His mouth closed over hers, hungry and possessive.

Brittany's resistance was dissolved in one powerful surge of molten heat. Her strength deserted her and left her clinging to Jake with unrestrained need.

All at once she knew why she'd missed so many chances during the evening to put Jake off. She'd been harboring a secret hope that he wouldn't allow it. She realized with sudden clarity that she wanted him to overcome her protests so that she wouldn't have to feel responsible for surrendering to him. But why shouldn't she surrender? Not one valid reason came to her, and she didn't care that Jake was about to break his vow of one-night celibacy. She'd been a fool to push him into offering such a promise in the first place. To shrink from being with Jake Mallory while he was around to be enjoyed was like hiding indoors throughout a perfect summer because eventually it would give way to winter.

As her tongue danced with his, Brittany pressed herself against him and felt the rigid promise of his body. A shudder of sweet anticipation rippled through her. Any moment now he would lift her in his arms and carry her to her bed . . . or the couch . . . or the living room carpet. It didn't matter where he took her, as long as he soothed the throbbing ache inside her.

Any moment now . . .

Three

"You're so delicious," Jake murmured when he paused so that they could catch their breath. "So sweet and soft and eager."

Oh, yes, Brittany thought as she gazed up at him with glazed, unfocused eyes. *She was eager. So what was he* waiting *for?*

Jake's hands glided upward over her back to her shoulders, coming to rest with his fingers on the nape of her neck and his thumbs caressing the delicate line of her jaw. "That mouth of yours has been driving me crazy all evening," he said, his voice hoarse. "Watching you during dinner was sheer torment." He bent to kiss one corner of her mouth, then the other. "Sweetheart, you have no idea how close you were to being seduced right there in the restaurant," he murmured, his warm breath mingling with hers. "If it hadn't been for that infernal promise of mine . . ." Sighing heavily, he contented himself with sliding his thumbs upward to stroke Brittany's full lower lip. As he traced the entire outline of her mouth, he watched her fathomless brown eyes darken almost to black and a flush creep over her skin.

Brittany's eyes widened as his words slowly sank in. All the time she'd been thinking he'd lost interest in her, he'd been on the brink of making love to her? Yet now that he had the chance, now that he'd been enough of a Svengali to drive all her objections right out of her mind, he was saying he *wouldn't* make love to her? The man was going to drive her insane. "Your promise?" she repeated. "You mean you . . . you intend to keep it?"

Her obvious shock and disappointment sent a rush of triumph surging through Jake like a potent aphrodisiac. He was tempted to change his mind. Oh, so tempted.

With an enormous effort of will, he said, "Of course I'm keeping my promise." He spoke as much to himself as to Brittany. "I don't make promises lightly."

Brittany searched his eyes, then removed her hands from around his neck and fisted them at her sides as she took a step back. "Then why did you kiss me, Jake? Are you . . . just trying to prove something?"

"Hey, sweetheart, a kiss *is* just a kiss," Jake said teasingly, taking one of her hands in both of his and uncurling her fingers one by one. As he touched his lips to her palm, it was all he could do not to drag her into his arms again and laugh with pure joy. He hadn't planned to turn the tables on Brittany this way, but that she seemed upset by his self-control did wonders for his confidence. "All I remember promising was not to let you lure me to the nearest bed, and I won't," he reminded her, then grew more serious. "I'm not trying to prove anything, Brittany. What I said a minute ago was the simple truth. Your sensuality is so instinctive, you don't realize that everything you do is exciting and arousing to me. I had to kiss you . . . and hold you . . . and touch you. I had to. But, sweetheart, the next time we make love will be when I know you can give yourself to me without any later regrets, when I'm sure you're ready to go all the way with me, in the deepest sense of the words."

Brittany felt her blood pulsing wildly as sheer panic caught her in its grip. "Just what *is* the deepest sense of those words?" she asked, pulling back her hand and turning to march into the living room. She began switching on lamps, ridding every nook and cranny of the shadows that encouraged intimacy. "I imagine you and I have very different interpretations."

"I have a pretty fair idea what *I* mean," Jake said quietly, leaning his shoulder against the wall at the room's entrance, his arms folded and one foot crossed over the other ankle in a nonchalant stance. "What's *your* interpretation?"

Brittany didn't answer right away. She was busy straightening knickknacks and magazines and coffee-table books that didn't need straightening.

Jake remained silent, deciding to play a waiting game.

During the standoff his glance quickly took in an interesting feature of Brittany's furnishings. Everything was scaled up, not down, despite her petite stature and feminine delicacy. There was nothing masculine about the place, but it was designed for comfort—a man's comfort. It was inviting to the body as well as to the eye.

Brittany endured the silence and Jake's fascinated scrutiny of her home as long as she could. "I'm trying to be sensible," she said as she took a plastic spritz bottle from the windowsill and began squirting water on the leaves of her plants. "I'm trying to avoid a situation where one or even both of us could get hurt. I'm being realistic."

"The hell you are," Jake growled, pushing himself off the wall and striding across the room. He took the spritz bottle from her and put it back on the windowsill, then grasped her by the shoulders while her mouth was still open in surprise. "There's nothing realistic about thinking you can force yourself *not* to feel something you *do* feel. There's nothing realistic about putting us both through all this frustration when you know we both want the same thing!"

Realizing he was about to kiss her again and obliterate her logic in another tide of sensation, Brittany said desperately, "But do we really want the same thing, Jake? I admit we both want to make love, but what happens later, when it's time for you to leave? I'm not up to having an affair with you whenever you happen to be in the same town or country or . . . or . . . *hemisphere*! I can't make love to you one day and wave good-bye the next, not knowing when or if I'll ever see you again."

"If?" Jake repeated with a start. He didn't think there was any way Brittany could know what a close call he'd had on his last assignment. She must have the crazy idea that danger was a regular feature of his existence. "Brittany, I'm an engineer, that's all. Not a soldier of fortune risking my neck in sniper-infested jungles." He hoped she would accept his reassurance. Sooner or later he would have to tell her about his recent adventures—and misadventures—but given what she'd just said, later seemed better than sooner.

Brittany tilted her head to one side and slanted him a puzzled look. "I only meant you might not choose to come back to me, Jake. I've never thought you were involved in anything life-threatening." Watching the play of emotion in Jake's eyes, she knew he was holding back something important. "Just where have you been during the past four months?" she asked. "Why have you lost weight? What is it about those months that you can't, or won't, talk about?

Jake stared at her for a moment, then pulled himself together and managed a grin. "Don't try to squirm out of this discussion by straying from the subject, sweetheart. We were talking about that inevitable moment when you'll give yourself to me without reservations. All the way, remember? You were supposed to be telling me what that loaded little phrase means to you. What's the matter, Brittany? Are you afraid to be honest with both of us?" He dipped his head to brush kisses over her forehead and temples. "Worried that we might turn out to want exactly the same things?"

Aware that Jake was determined to distract her from her questions about the mysterious period after he'd left Australia, Brittany managed not to succumb totally. Even as he grazed his lips down to her throat and touched his tongue to a pulse spot that had begun throbbing wildly, she focused firmly on her mounting outrage instead of her heightening desire. How could he ask her to trust him with her whole heart and soul when he wouldn't tell her something as basic as where he'd spent the past four months of his life? And he'd said *she* wasn't honest? How honest was it for him to imply he wanted more than a brief affair when his track record for any kind of permanence was nil?

She decided he was pulling some kind of bluff. She also decided to call him on it.

With a huskiness she didn't have to pretend—Jake's kisses were heating her blood to the boiling point no matter how she tried to ignore them—Brittany asked softly, "Is it possible we *do* want the same things, Jake? Am I reading you all wrong?"

"Could be," he murmured lazily, his attention concentrated more on what he was doing than what she was saying.

"How strange," Brittany said as his teasing lips sent a shudder through her. "I'd never have dreamed we might feel the same way about the . . . well, the basics. Such as my need for roots. A sense of . . . of connectedness, if you know what I mean. It's important to me to be part of a community, caring about people and having them care about me. . . ."

"You're a nest builder," Jake put in helpfully as his lips followed the line of her throat down to her collarbone, his hands going to the buttons of her coat and deftly undoing them. "It bothers you that I've spent my whole life in free flight."

"Ex-exactly," Brittany said, battling the instinct to reach up and thread her fingers through his hair. Somehow she kept her palms flattened against his chest, poised to push him away. "Do you realize I'm thirty-one?"

"Really? So old?" Jake drawled. His kisses moved downward, tracing the wide V of her neckline and the upper slopes of her breasts, leaving a trail of fire. "You're remarkably well preserved, Kitten. Firm, smooth, silky . . ."

"You may laugh," Brittany cut in, though neither of them seemed to be laughing. And she wished he wouldn't call her by that name. It had a strange effect on her. "But the fact is, my biological clock is ticking fast these days."

Jake straightened up and gazed into Brittany's

eyes, his grip on her shoulders tightening. "Your biological clock?"

His expression was inscrutable, but Brittany had faith in her ticking-biological-clock routine. It had worked as an effective man repellent before, when she'd used it on far more domesticated males than Jake Mallory. "The Mr. Right I've begun looking for might not be glamorous or exciting," she went on in a spurt of creativity, "but he'll be prepared to meet mortgage payments every single month for twenty years. He'll carry life insurance, drive a family-sized car, and truly enjoy spending his Saturday afternoons at the supermarket." Gaining confidence as she went along, she smiled again and playfully walked the fingers of one hand up Jake's chest, a sexy gesture deliberately meant as a ludicrous contrast with her next words. "He'll be a reliable husband and a . . . an *involved* father, the kind who'll learn how to change diapers and walk a screaming baby until its colic goes away, who'll be patient about telling endless bedtime stories to three-year-olds." Brushing the backs of her fingers over Jake's jawline and feeling a muscle twitch convulsively, Brittany went straight for the jugular: "Do you think you could fill the bill, Jake?" she cooed.

"Diapers," he recited in a monotone. "Colic. Bedtime stories." His brows quirked upward. "Anything more?"

Ignoring her perverse disappointment at the obvious success of her ploy, Brittany smiled and nodded. "Oh, a lot more. But do you really want me to go on and on about things like . . . oh, how my dream man will enjoy spending his annual two-week vacation driving to Disneyland? How he'll be the soul of patience when the kids start whining because they're bored in the car?" Good grief, Brittany thought, she was scaring *herself*! Time to wrap it up. "Jake, I admit we're . . . well, terribly excited about each other right now. But that sort of thing can't last. Marriage is based on common goals, not fleeting passion. And marriage is all I'm interested in. Marriage, children, picket fences . . . the whole picture. That's what I mean by 'all the way.' If you mean the same thing and feel the same way, maybe we do have a chance together."

The muscle in Jake's jaw worked furiously. Brittany fixed her gaze on it, unable to meet his eyes as she braced herself for his exit line, telling herself she'd done the right thing. The pain in her heart, the squeezing of her lungs until she could hardly breathe, and the sick sensation in her stomach would go away eventually.

No, it wouldn't! she realized too late, wondering if she could backtrack and tell Jake she hadn't meant a word of what she'd just said.

The trouble was, she wasn't certain her story had been a complete fiction. Until she'd met Jake, she'd wanted nothing but her independence and a successful career, at least for a few more years of unwedded bliss. Her parents enjoyed such a wonderful relationship—in sharp contrast to so many miserable marriages she'd observed—she'd been holding out for the same near perfection. And an early disappointment in the love department had left her very careful. But her biological clock actually *had* started ticking, and Jake was the man who'd wound it!

Suddenly, just when Brittany thought Jake was going to spout whatever excuse he'd come up with for the quickest about-face in romantic history, he rested his forehead against hers and dissolved into quiet laughter.

Bewildered by his reaction, Brittany glowered at him, though it was difficult to give someone a fierce look at such close range.

"Sweetheart, you're adorable," Jake said at last.

Brittany's frown deepened as it occurred to her that she must have overplayed her hand. She should have known that Jake required more subtlety than the average amorous male.

Finally raising his head and cradling her face between his hands, he said in a soft caress, "No wonder I couldn't get you out of my mind, Brittany Thomas." Gazing at her, his eyes gradually losing their glints of humor to turn dark and searching, he went on quietly, "However crazy my life was—and for those four months you're so curious about it was pretty rough—the vision of you kept me going. You were like my personal patron saint, even though you'd deserted me long before my hour of need."

Brittany immediately forgot everything but her concern for him. "Jake, what are you saying? Just how crazy was your life? Why did you need a . . . a patron saint? What hour of need? Where have you been, dammit?"

Jake sighed heavily. Telling Brittany about his experiences wasn't going to advance his cause with her, but he'd left himself no choice. "I went from Australia to the Middle East, at first on a series of engineering assignments but ultimately as a reluctant guest of an obscure little bunch of terrorists," he answered in a monotone, as if the lack of expression in his voice would soften the effect of the words.

As Brittany blanched and her eyes rounded with shock, Jake quickly added, "It was no big deal, sweetheart. I was more annoyed than worried. A gang of . . . of kids, really, snatched me right out of the company limo because I was careless, but I got away a few weeks later because they were even more careless. Or maybe they weren't. They were amateurs, and I half suspect they arranged for me to get away because they got cold feet."

"Dear heaven," Brittany whispered. "You could have been killed, and I'd never have known. Nobody would have thought to tell me. . . ." She blinked, appalled by the bleak prospect of a world without Jake Mallory wandering around somewhere, even if he wasn't with her. "Were you . . . hurt?" she asked, unable to use a stronger word.

He shook his head and grinned. "Nothing as dramatic as torture, if that's what you're thinking. I was roughed up a bit when I tried to resist being taken, that's all. The worst thing I had to put up with was day after day of inactivity and tedium. But even the enforced solitude had its plus side, because it gave me a chance for a lot of overdue thinking. I've never been a reflective person, but once the process started, I couldn't seem to turn it off. I looked at my life and saw the empty places in it. I thought about you. About us. About why two people who'd managed to get so close so quickly had lost each other. I vowed I'd find out as soon as I got the chance. And here I am."

"Jake, how can you treat such a shattering experience so lightly?" Brittany asked, unable to get past the horror of knowing what he'd been through while she'd been picturing him wining and dining beautiful women in exotic places. "How did such a dreadful thing happen? Where were you? Why did those people pick on you to . . . ?"

"It's a long story," Jake cut in, eager to drop the subject. "Let's leave the gory details for some other time, shall we?"

"But . . ."

"Not now," Jake insisted softly. "Let me just look at you for another minute before I go."

As his fingers trailed slowly downward over her throat, his touch light and evocative. Brittany found her intense curiosity nudged aside by a profound yearning. She recalled the night when Jake had stroked her whole body. Her back had arched instinctively; her skin felt wonderously alive to his touch as he smoothed his palms over every inch of her.

All at once Brittany realized that Jake's arms were going around her and his mouth was covering hers again, at first so gently he brought tears to her eyes, then with deepening possessiveness, his tongue coaxing her lips apart and his hands moving over her back, molding her against him, pressing on the base of her spine so that she felt his desire and remembered how it was to be filled by him. A soft moan escaped her throat. Her arms stole around his neck. Her will, once again, was bending to his.

When she heard an oddly muffled ringing in the distance, Brittany wanted to ignore it. If someone was phoning her, it was probably a wrong number. Then it occurred to her that the ringing was constant, not like a phone at all. She still wanted to dismiss the sound, deciding it was just part of Jake's effect on her. The earth moved when he was near. Why wouldn't she hear bells?

But when Jake released her mouth, raised his head, and frowned, she knew he was hearing the noise as well.

After a moment of confusion Brittany figured out what was happening. "It's nothing to be concerned about," she murmured, all her resistance to Jake forgotten. Exploring the myriad possibilities of erotic pleasure with him seemed like a wonderful idea. "The building next door has been having trouble with its fire-alarm system all week," she explained, tracing the long column of his spine with feathery fingertips.

Catching his breath on a sharp groan, Jake reached back to clamp his fingers around Brittany's wrists, brought her arms to her sides, and gave her a quick hug as he dropped a kiss to the tip of her nose. He wanted Brittany, but only when she was ready emotionally as well as physically. "Just a phony fire alarm?" he said, mustering a roguish grin. "Whew! That's a relief. For a minute there I thought it was your biological clock going off."

Before Brittany could come up with a response, Jake was gone, the door quietly clicking shut behind him.

She stared after him in impotent outrage mingled with yawning despair. For all she knew, she would never see him again. He might check out of the hotel and leave town first thing in the morning, without even saying good-bye.

It was better this way, Brittany told herself. A quick, clean ending to something that never should have even begun.

But dammit, she thought as a sob caught in her throat, it didn't *feel* better.

Cold showers were overrated as libido deadeners, Jake mused as he sipped fresh grapefruit juice and waited for his poached-egg-on-toast in the Trellis Room, the cozy restaurant tucked into one corner of the Somerset's lobby. He'd stood under a chilly blast of water the night before, then tried the treatment again after he'd opened his eyes to the first light of dawn and the endless ache of wanting Brittany.

He wondered if he should have made love to her after all, if he could have bound her to him emotionally with the power of physical intimacy. Yet he knew he had to do a lot of thinking before he took such a step. Brittany was so very vulnerable, it was up to him to protect her from the likes of Jake Mallory.

Accustomed to worldly women who could take care of themselves, Jake had decided he had to be super-cautious with Brittany. Her transparent diapers-and-colic scare tactics had revealed some essential truths about her, whether she realized it or not. She was operating on two warring instincts: her desire for him versus her sense of self-preservation. A sometime love affair wouldn't be enough for Brittany, and he hadn't offered anything more because he was operating on his own instincts—the simple need to make her belong to him. He hadn't planned what to do with her once she was his. What he really wanted was to be able to scoop her up, tuck her into his pocket, and take her wherever he went, but he had the distinct impression Brittany wouldn't go for pocket-dwelling.

Sensing a presence at his elbow, Jake reluctantly put his private debate on hold and looked up.

"You've just *got* to be Mount Rushmore," an attractive white-haired woman in a violet linen suit said as she smiled down at him.

Surprised he hadn't noticed her approach, Jake pushed back his chair and got to his feet. "I beg your pardon?"

"A gentleman. How nice," she said with a soft laugh, then extended her hand. "You're Jake Mallory, aren't you?"

"Yes, I am," Jake answered. He gently gripped her outstretched hand, but the lady had such a regal manner, he almost felt he should lift her fingers to his lips, "You have me at a disadvantage, ma'am."

"Sorry about that Mount Rushmore remark," she said warmly. "Blame our desk clerk. The Somerset is such a small hotel, its staff and guests tend to be like family, and therefore as gossipy. Trudy told me about our newest arrival, and her description was so perfect, I couldn't resist teasing you with it. I understand, by the way, that you and my lovely young manager are acquainted."

"Oh, so you're Helena," Jake blurted out, then hastily corrected himself. "I mean, you must be Mrs. Danforth."

"Helena," she said, her sapphire eyes alight with surprise and curiosity. "But how did you know?"

"Brittany talked about you at length over dinner last night. You came off better in Brittany's portrait than I did in Trudy's, though," he remarked with a grin. "Mount Rushmore?"

"As in 'unique, rugged, and worth looking at,'" Helena said firmly.

Laughing, Jake indicated the chair across from his. "Is it acceptable for the newest member of the Somerset's family to ask the matriarch to join me?"

"Acceptable and accepted," she answered, sitting down and settling in for breakfast.

For the next half hour Jake knew he was being checked out by the commanding little woman, though he was grilled with great charm.

By the time he and Helena were lingering over a second cup of coffee and a lovely conversation, Jake had reason to hope he'd passed muster. She was doing more than chatting amiably. She was dropping bits of information to help him in his pursuit of Brittany.

Chasing a reluctant woman wasn't his style, he

told himself, even if her mentor was playing match-maker. And it wouldn't be right for him to push his way into Brittany's life unless he was certain . . .

One searing truth put a sudden halt to Jake's internal discussion. To lose Brittany without doing everything in his power to win her was unthinkable.

He made a mental note of the time Helena glanced at her watch and casually mentioned that Brittany would be finishing up her regular morning walk in the park or on the seawall—her normal routine after a quick breakfast at the Starting Gate, a diner a few blocks from the hotel. "I do wish Brittany wouldn't strike out on her own for her promenades when there aren't many other people around," Helena said with a little shake of her head. "Some dreadfully seedy characters tend to gravitate to Stanley Park overnight. It was different when Casey went with her. . . ."

"Casey?" Jake said sharply, his insides wrenching with startling possessiveness.

Helena's brows arched, and her lips curved in a tiny smile.

Jake stared at her, shocked by the intensity of his reaction. He cleared his throat. "Would this Casey be female?" he asked, belatedly trying to sound off-hand, "Or . . . male?"

"Let's just say Casey hasn't been up to going with Brittany lately thanks to an unexpected bout of all-day morning sickness," Helena answered, her eyes dancing.

"That's a shame," Jake said with a sudden grin that faded as he realized he was being insensitive about Brittany's friend. "I mean, it really is a shame. Maybe there's something I can do."

"Such as joining Brittany for her walk?" Helena

said with an innocent smile. "Why, what a lovely idea, Jake. I'm so glad you thought of it."

"That wasn't what I meant, but of course I'd . . ." Jake broke off, belatedly understanding that Helena had given him her blessing.

Grinning conspiratorially, he nodded. "Early-morning walks," he murmured. "Oddly enough, I happen to like them myself."

Four

Taking his cue from Helena, Jake decided that the wisest way to get close to Brittany without making her feel pressured would be to arrange a few accidental meetings with her.

To go right to the Starting Gate would be too obvious, so the best alternative was to stage a chance encounter somewhere in the vastness of Stanley Park and its many paths. A woman walking alone in the early hours of the day would be inclined to stick to the seawall surrounding the park, he reasoned. He would do the same and hope for the best.

On his first outing, the morning after his talk with Helena, he enjoyed a brisk stroll despite not seeing Brittany. The long spell of his captivity, when the food had been indifferent and the opportunity for exercise limited, had left him with a physical lethargy he was determined to shake. It occurred to him that a few weeks spent rebuilding his strength in a laid-back city like Vancouver couldn't hurt.

Cupid smiled more kindly on Jake that afternoon.

Returning to the Somerset after an afternoon workout—not at a fancy health club but at an old-fashioned gym where boxers and other serious athletes honed their bodies—he parked his rental car in the hotel parking lot and entered the lobby through a side door.

His heart skipped a beat as he saw a flash of buttercup yellow and realized it was Brittany in a crisp cotton suit, heading toward the door at her usual force-ten velocity. She was too engrossed in giving last-minute instructions to Trudy on her way past the front desk to notice Jake walking toward her—or to see him alter his own course just enough to place himself directly in her path. He felt only a twinge of guilt for causing the inevitable collision. The end justified the means.

Brittany barreled into him, and as Jake wrapped his arms around her, he couldn't suppress a satisfied smile.

Brittany was aghast at her clumsiness. "Oh! I'm sorry!" she said the minute she caught her breath. "Please, forgive . . ." Her eyes widened, and her voice turned to a whisper. "Jake."

He felt her body soften instinctively against his and watched her lips part, her gaze luminous with sudden desire. "I forgive you," he said magnanimously.

Brittany stared up at him, flushed and gripped by tremors of excitement she was certain Jake could feel rippling through her. She'd known since morning that he hadn't left town. She'd checked the hotel guest list. But he hadn't called or sought her out all day, so she assumed he'd given up on her.

Several seconds passed as Jake considered covering Brittany's lovely mouth with his and tasting the sweetness he'd become addicted to. Realizing that her professional image might suffer from such a public display, however, he resisted the temptation. "I was hoping I'd bump into you," he said with a grin.

Brittany laughed shakily. "I think you have it backward. I'm the one who bumped into you, remember?"

"That's right. So you did," Jake replied, managing to keep a straight face. Encouraged by the warmth of her yielding body, he added, "Have dinner with me tonight?"

He regretted his rash invitation as Brittany hastily extricated herself from his arms. "I mustn't, Jake. I mean, I can't. That is, I . . ."

"You can stop tripping over your tongue," he cut in, smiling stiffly. "If you can't, you can't. No big deal."

"Oh," Brittany said in a small voice, then straightened her shoulders and lifted her chin. "Well, I'd better be on my way. I'm due at a Sea Festival committee meeting and I'm running late."

Brittany's explanation of where she was headed pleased Jake. She "mustn't" go out with him, but she still felt she had to tell him where she was going. His smile grew more genuine. "See you around," he said lightly.

As Brittany nodded, mumbled another apology for bumping into him, and hurried away, Jake silently berated himself for asking her to have dinner with him. So much for easing up on the pressure. But Brittany had a way of short-circuiting his thinking processes. His body still tingled from the electricity he'd absorbed from hers; his chest ached to feel her breasts crushed against it; his loins were hot with the visceral memory of her perfect fit.

He managed a breezy greeting for Trudy as he strode past her toward the elevators, and he exchanged small talk with another of the hotel's guests on the way up to his floor. But perspiration was beading Jake's forehead by the time he let himself into his room, a lingering reaction to the moment of contact with Brittany's soft promise.

It was time for some transcendental meditation, he decided, glad he'd acquired his personal mantra during a stay in India a couple of years before. It had served him well ever since.

But first he stripped off his clothes and headed for the bathroom. Perhaps a second cold shower would prove more successful than the first.

Jake's second seawall expedition offered a tangy ocean breeze, warm sunlight dappling the waters of English Bay, and a growing appreciation for the sheer wonder of being free to walk wherever he liked.

It was hard for him to believe he'd escaped from captivity in a depressing desert village just three weeks earlier. After a quick debriefing with the State Department in Washington, an emotional but short reunion with his parents in San Diego, and a pit stop at his office in Santa Barbara to check in with his assistant, he'd slept for two days straight. Then he'd boarded a plane for Vancouver, and as soon as he'd landed, had headed for the small hotel where, he'd found out, Brittany worked. He was glad he'd made the trip, not only because he'd discovered she still felt something for him. Apart from the constant tension of unfulfilled desire for her, he was more relaxed then he'd been in a long time. He could feel the rapid regeneration of his body and the soothing of the frayed edges of his spirit.

Drawing closer to the Somerset, Jake broke into an easy lope.

He wasn't lucky enough to see Brittany in the lobby this time, but Helena was there, so he made a date with her for tea in the Trellis Room later in the morning. Then he paused to check with Trudy for messages and traded a few corny jokes with her.

Without consciously trying to make it happen, he was beginning to feel like part of the Somerset family. And oddly enough, he liked that feeling.

It was midnight, and Brittany was dressed for bed in her favorite cream silk nightshirt, styled like a man's pajama top and comfortably roomy. She was sitting cross-legged on the oversize sofa in her apartment, her eyes closed as she listened to a Bach concerto. She'd read somewhere that baroque music calmed the nerves, cleared away the cobwebs of a confused mind, and induced sleep—something to do with alpha waves, apparently.

She didn't care whether it involved *tidal* waves, as long as it helped her wash a certain man right out of her hair!

Jake was tormenting her. He'd invaded her territory, occupied her mind, and besieged her dreams.

As far as she knew, he had no reason to stay in Vancouver. He certainly didn't seem to be sticking around to pursue her. Yet he'd told Trudy he had no immediate plans to leave. He was going to enjoy an overdue vacation, he'd said. Trudy had been delighted. Another victim of Jake Mallory's lethal charm.

Even Helena wasn't immune. Brittany had spotted her boss sharing tea with Jake in the Trellis Room that morning, and later in the day Helena had stopped by Brittany's office just long enough to utter the very words Brittany had dreaded hearing. Jake reminded Helena of her beloved David, not in looks but in personality and character. "A rare breed," Helena had said, then sighed. "The kind of man a woman can trust. A man who'll be her friend, not just her lover. A man she can count on."

Sure she can, if she can find him on some remote South Sea Island or at the top of a Himalayan mountain, Brittany thought, getting up to stalk over to her tape deck and switch off Bach, who wasn't doing a thing for her peace of mind.

She stepped out onto her balcony and stood with her arms folded on the railing, breathing in the tang of salt air mingled with the fresh scent of evergreen from the trees and shrubbery lining the streets below. A cool breeze brushed her cheek and swirled playfully around her bare legs, teasing at the hem of her nightshirt and rippling the silk material so that it caressed her skin as tantalizingly as Jake's lips and tongue would if he were . . .

"That does it," Brittany said, whirling to go back inside. "I give up. I can't fight this thing anymore." She marched straight to the phone, picked up the receiver, and started to punch out the number of the Somerset.

She hung up just before hitting the last digit. It was midnight, she reminded herself. Jake might be asleep. After his ordeal in the Middle East, he needed time to recuperate. It wouldn't be right to disturb his rest.

Glaring at the phone, Brittany muttered, "Why not? He's disturbing *my* rest." Besides, would he mind a late-night phone call from a woman admitting her capitulation?

She bit down on her lower lip. *What if he'd lost interest? Worse, what if he had a capitulating woman in his bed already?*

Recoiling from the phone as if it had turned into a cobra, Brittany retreated to her bedroom and crawled between the crisp sheets, deciding to stare up at the ceiling until sheer boredom put her to sleep.

Jake's third seawall expedition brought no better result than the first two. He told himself to keep the faith. Maybe he'd absorbed too much of the mysticism of the east over the years, but he believed he was meant to win Brittany, and if an early-morning rendezvous was part of fate's plan, it would happen.

If it didn't happen, he thought with a wry smile, he would come up with a new plan. A more direct, aggressive one. Mysticism or no mysticism, he was an American male with only so much patience. He would determine his own fate.

A busload of tourists from Australia had arrived at the Somerset when Jake returned from a tennis match against a lawyer he'd met at the gym. The Aussies were milling around the lobby, a few of them sitting on the stairway talking volubly among themselves about the scenic drive from Seattle.

As Jake stepped onto the elevator, he was followed by several of the newcomers. He smiled, enjoying their accents and their exuberance. He'd liked the people Down Under during the time he'd spent there. They were a no-nonsense, fun-loving crowd.

The doors were shutting when one of the men in the group stuck out his arm to stop them. "Going up, plenty of room," he said jovially.

Jake, at the back of the elevator, tilted his head to peer past the Amazonian blond woman directly in front of him. His pulse skipped several beats as he saw Brittany urging the Aussie to let the doors shut, saying she would take the next car or negotiate her way up the stairs. Timing was everything, Jake thought with a prickle of irritation, and this particular timing was rotten. What a break it would have been for him to be caught alone with Brittany in an elevator, even for a minute or two.

The big Aussie cheerfully refused to budge, and as his companions rearranged themselves to show Brittany that there was lots of space for her, she gave in with a smile. But she stopped dead as the Amazon in front of Jake moved to one side—with just a little subtle nudging from him—leaving Brittany only one place to stand.

"Come on, lass, let's go," the self-appointed elevator operator boomed. "All the way in now! Don't get your knickers caught in the doors!"

Brittany gave Jake a hesitant smile, submitted to the inevitable, and edged into the space just in front of him.

As she turned to face the front, Brittany found herself wondering whether Jake could have arranged for this situation. It didn't seem possible, but his twinkling grin was giving her pause. And heart flutters. Of course the way he looked in tennis whites, with his skin regaining its bronze glow, his muscles rippling with strength under his formfitting T-shirt, and his long legs a study in masculine beauty, wasn't much help. Until she'd met Jake, she'd never dreamed she was capable of such lust.

"Could you back up a little, miss?" one of the smaller men in the group said, shouldering his way from the corner to center front. "A touch of claustophobia," he explained with an apologetic smile. "I'm used to the wide-open spaces of Oz. From now on I'll use the stairs, but this time I think I can bear up if I'm near the doors. You don't mind?"

"Of course not," Brittany said, swallowing hard as she made room for him by moving back even closer to Jake. She felt the familiar heat that emanated from the whole length of his body, and she half expected—or half-wished—his hands would begin traveling surreptitiously over her.

But his hands remained in his pockets, intensifying her frustrated desire.

Behind her, Jake smiled and made a mental note that he owed a pint or two to the unprepossessing little Australian who'd picked up instantly on the man-to-man eye signals Jake had slanted him in a silent request for a little cooperation. The claustrophobia routine had been inspired.

The elevator stopped on the second floor with a slight lurch Brittany had never noticed before. As she leaned involuntarily into Jake, she was aware immediately of unmistakable proof that he still wanted her.

"This is my stop," she said with a catch in her voice. Unable to resist turning to glance at Jake over her shoulder as she left the elevator, she saw his innocent smile and wondered if her imagination was working overtime.

No, she told herself. When their bodies had touched, she'd felt what she'd felt.

Surely he would call her that night. If he did, she would say yes. Whatever he suggested, she would say yes.

She wouldn't call him, though. He'd looked rather too pleased with himself on that elevator.

Jake finished another cold shower and another session of meditation without transcending the needs of his body one iota, so he decided to try a workout on the heavy bag at the gym.

The temptation to call down to Brittany's office to ask her out again was compelling, but he didn't want her to get into the habit of saying no to him, and he wasn't sure she was ready to say yes. If she'd answered his last invitation with only "I can't," he'd have assumed her meeting was going to take up her evening and been more inclined to try again. But she'd started her refusal with, "I mustn't," which was a whole other problem.

No, he decided, he wouldn't call her. He would keep trying the seawall for another day or two.

The heavy bag helped settle Jake down a little. So did the speed bag. And the push-ups, the sit-ups, and the laps in the pool.

Unfortunately the more Jake pushed his body, the more aware of it he became, the more attuned to its demands.

He was leaving the gym when he ran into a building contractor who'd hired him for several Vancouver jobs in the past.

"Jake, what are you doing in this neck of the woods?" Les Wildman asked. "The last I heard, you were checking out military installations in some Middle East hot spot."

"You heard right, so as soon as I finished that stint, I came here to cool off," Jake answered. Then he surprised himself by adding that he was open to any contracts that might be up for grabs in the Vancouver area. Until that moment his vague goal had been to conquer Brittany's heart so thoroughly, she would go with him to any corner of the world.

What had brought on this idea of staying in *her* corner?

Les jumped at the suggestion, pinning Jake down to dinner and a serious discussion that very evening. They would meet in the lobby of the Somerset at six.

It was almost a relief for Jake that the question of whether or not to risk asking Brittany out was settled for that night.

He was waiting for Les in the hotel's sitting area when he glanced up from the paper he was scanning and saw Brittany bounding down the stairs, stopping on the bottom step to talk to the housekeeping manager. As usual Jake's pulse rate accelerated like a race car in the Indy, and the blood in his veins was as hotly explosive as high-octane fuel.

It struck him that his chance-encounter scenario was having considerably more success in the lobby of the Somerset than on the seawall, though the brief meetings at the hotel were as frustrating as they were pleasurable. They didn't *lead* anywhere.

Brittany was absorbed in a discussion with the head of hotel housekeeping, and all Jake could do was enjoy looking at her, watching the way her beautiful hair gleamed under the light of an overhead chandelier and moved with a life of its own each time she gave one of her vigorous nods or shakes of the head.

She was so earnest, he thought affectionately. So involved in her work. So attentive to every detail of the Somerset's operation. She treated the hotel like a work of living art; she was like the conductor of a symphony, the director of a fine film.

Jake realized with a slight shock that he hadn't given serious consideration to the importance of Brittany's work in her life. To him a contract was something he took pride in fulfilling with efficiency and excellence, but he couldn't remember the last time he'd felt a real connection to any given project, and it had been years since he'd built anything other than his own reputation as a troubleshooter for other people's dreams.

Perhaps he'd been missing something.

And perhaps his subconscious had listened more closely to Brittany than he'd been aware. Why else would he have told Les he was interested in Vancouver contracts?

Across the lobby Brittany laughed at whatever the housekeeper had said to her.

Jake caught his breath, *God, how he loved Brittany's silvery laughter.* It hit him for the first time that the memory of that sweet, rippling sound had sustained him through countless despairing moments.

Hardly aware of what he was doing, Jake got to his feet and started toward her, his careful plan forgotten in the simple need to reach out to her.

Brittany turned and saw him, as if she'd felt the burning intensity of his gaze. Her face lit up, and Jake's heart lurched. But in the very next second her expression clouded over, her dazzling smile diminishing to a polite facsimile as she nodded a silent greeting. Then she pivoted on her heel and raced up the stairs as if he'd frightened her.

Jake stopped in his tracks, not sure what had happened. Had he grown vampire's fangs?

"Sorry I'm late," he heard a moment later at his shoulder.

Turning, Jake stared blankly at Les Wildman.

"I got stuck in a traffic jam," Les explained. "I'm starved. Any special place you want to eat, Jake? I hear the food in the dining room here is terrific, but I found this great Indonesian place. . . ."

"Indonesian," Jake said. Glancing at the empty staircase, he murmured, "Indonesian sounds perfect."

The next morning when Jake got ready for his walk, he was strangely confident of success. He felt it in every fiber of his being as he pulled on his denim cutoffs and a white T-shirt. Ironic, he thought. After Brittany's inexplicable flight from him the day before, he wasn't certain he wanted to meet her on the seawall. She might not welcome his company.

The day was perfect, the sky so clear, there wasn't a single misty veil obscuring the Coastal Mountains or the row upon row of white summits behind them. The air was crisp but softened by a promise of coming warmth, and even the songs of birds flitting around in the park's trees and shrubbery seemed charged with special excitement.

Jake was halfway around the peninsula and moving at a fairly good clip when two men jogged down from the roadway above onto the seawall some distance in front of him.

They looked harmless, Jake thought as he automatically sized them up—a habit that had helped him avoid a few tight spots over the years. The one time he'd relaxed his vigilance, he'd paid dearly for the lapse.

One of the joggers was blond and tanned, the other dark-haired and winter-pale. Neither was especially large. Jake suspected they jogged strictly for cosmetic reasons, not to train their bodies to be ready for fight-or-flight situations.

Definitely harmless, he decided, wondering at the same time how long it would be before he stopped anticipating trouble from strangers.

Moments later his attention was drawn to a petite, feminine figure approaching in the distance beyond the joggers. The woman's hot-pink shorts and electric-blue sweatshirt looked like something Brittany might wear, and her chestnut hair was exactly the right color, even if the bouncy ponytail perched off center on top of her head was unfamiliar to Jake. But what tipped him off was her arm-swinging, eat-up-the-pavement stride.

Jake kept his pace steady.

He couldn't help smiling when he saw Brittany wave to a grizzled derelict standing on the beach below, rubbing the sleep out of his eyes as he folded up the newspapers and cardboard that must have been his bed overnight.

Without slowing her pace, Brittany slid a small backpack around to the front of her body and took an apple from it. Then she closed up the pack and flipped it to her back again.

The old man gave her a gap-toothed grin as she tossed him the apple, a routine that seemed familiar to both of them.

Trust Brittany, Jake thought, to do something thoughtful for a person others would pretend not to see.

He was still a fair distance from her when he saw the two joggers ahead of him slow down, nod to each other, then stop in their tracks, blocking Brittany's path.

Jake frowned, but told himself Brittany probably knew the men. He was in Vancouver, not Beirut or Baghdad.

But he saw her falter, and she didn't wave to the pair, or speak, or show any other sign of recognition.

One of them extended his hand and crooked a finger at her.

She shook her head, stood still for a moment, then started walking slowly backward, a strategy Jake considered singularly ineffective.

The joggers followed, matching her step for step.

Suddenly Brittany changed tactics and shot forward, aiming straight ahead in an attempt to barrel through the space between the two men.

Jake had seen enough. He broke into a dead run just as Brittany found out that her aggressiveness hadn't worked.

Five

Racing along the seawall, Jake felt fear and anger rip through him as he saw the men grab Brittany, each of them looping an arm though hers and lifting her straight up.

She was so panicky, her feet kept going as if she were riding an invisible airborne bicycle.

Jake was tempted to shout to let Brittany know he was on the way, but he wanted to surprise her captors. They didn't look like much to worry about, but it was best to be careful. Besides, she probably wouldn't hear him if he did yell. She was talking a mile a minute, first to one man, then the other, then the first again, her head swiveling from side to side like a spectator's at a close tennis match.

Jake clenched his teeth. If Brittany was trying to bluster her way out of the situation, she wasn't having much success. She was being carried up the low rise beside the seawall toward the road, where a car was parked.

His stomach twisted into a knot, even though he knew he had plenty of time to keep her from being pushed into the car and whisked away. The thought of what could have happened to her consumed him with rage. Exploding in a burst of speed, he was homing in on his quarry within seconds.

Sprinting closer, he heard the two men laughing as Brittany nagged them like a teacher berating a couple of naughty schoolboys: "You put me down this instant, you . . . you degenerates! I said no, and I *meant* no, dammit! Why do you want me, anyway? I keep telling you I'm no good, and I'm not kidding! I'm *laughable*, and that's the truth!"

Jake decided she must be in a state of witless terror if claiming ineptitude was the only defense she could come up with. But her nonstop nattering was enough of a diversion to let him get within reach without being noticed. Seizing each of her attackers by the side of the neck, he squeezed just hard enough to let them know he meant business and knew what he was doing.

As they jerked to a halt—still keeping Brittany suspended a few inches off the ground—they tried to turn their heads enough to see him, gaping in astonishment. Brittany did the same, and Jake gave her a tight smile. "Remind me to give you some self-defense pointers, will you?" he said with feigned calm. "Scoldings rarely work, even if you're very, very cross."

"Jake!" she gasped over her shoulder. "Where did you come from?"

He didn't answer. He had a more immediate matter on his mind. "Gentlemen," he said softly, "put the lady down, then let go of her arms. And be gentle with her, or I'll have all the excuse I need to ram your heads together."

Brittany was lowered slowly and with great caution to the ground.

"Um . . . it's not what it looks like, mister," the dark-haired jogger said as he released his hold on Brittany's arm.

The blond one let her go, then jerked himself free and whirled on Jake. "What's with you, fella? Who the hell do you think you are?"

"You're about to find out, pal," Jake answered, dropping the other man and pulling back his arm for the kind of solid punch he was aching to deliver.

Galvanized into action, Brittany leapt at Jake's arm to deflect the blow. "Jake, it's all right! They don't mean any harm!" she cried, then connected with what felt like an iron bar and let out a groan as the wind was knocked out of her.

Jake was horrified, though he was sure he hadn't hurt her. She'd collided with the side of his arm, not with his fist. "Are you all right, sweetheart?" he demanded, grasping her shoulders to steady her.

She nodded weakly. "I . . . I think so," she managed to answer despite struggling to catch her breath.

"Would somebody please tell me who this guy is?" the blond jogger said. Now ashen-faced, he sounded less belligerent than before. "Is he a friend of yours, Britt?"

Even more shaken than his intended victim, Jake ignored the man and spoke sternly to Brittany. "Don't you ever, *ever* pull a stunt like that again, understand? Don't get in my way when I'm . . ."

"About to demolish somebody?" she cut in.

"I wasn't going to demolish anybody. I thought I'd implant the idea that it's not nice to manhandle ladies, that's all. What was going on here, anyway?" It dawned on Jake that one of the joggers had called Brittany by name. "Do you know these characters?"

Suddenly struck by the low humor of the situation, Brittany couldn't resist saying, "I've never seen these men before in my life."

"Britt!" they both exploded at once, their expressions horrified.

As she saw Jake's brows draw together in a straight, forbidding line, Brittany relented. "Actually these two dopes are friends of mine."

"Friends?" Jake repeated.

She rolled her eyes. "I know. Isn't it awful, the riffraff we have to put up with because of our jobs?"

"Brittany," Jake said with a warning in his tone, "start explaining, and I mean now! I have a feeling I just made a fool of myself, but I'd like to be sure before I start offering apologies."

"All right, but there's no need for you to apologize for anything." She smiled up at him, belatedly realizing that if she'd been in real trouble, Jake would have been there to rescue her—and he'd have been more than up to the challenge. Assailed by an overwhelming temptation to nestle against his solid frame and feel the strength of his arms enfolding her, she added softly, "In fact if you do apologize, I'll never forgive you."

As he lost himself in her shining eyes, Jake had to steel himself against the instantaneous response of his loins. "I'm waiting," he said with exaggerated patience. "What just happened here?"

Startled from her dreamy lapse, Brittany began by making unceremonious introductions. Nodding toward Jake and then the dark-haired man, she said, "Jake Mallory, Fred Willoughby. Fred is sales director at the Pacific Inn and first-baseman for the Hotel Hotshots slo-pitch team. The gentleman whose face you were about to turn into a level surface is Larry Armstrong, assistant manger at the Lions Gate Towers and right-fielder for . . ." She paused and slanted Armstrong a questioning look. "Or is it left field, Larry?"

"Right," he answered tersely, still keeping a wary eye on Jake.

"Right field, or right correct?" she asked for no reason she could think of except that she was extremely rattled.

"Right field, but does it matter?" Larry said with obvious exasperation, finally offering her his full attention.

She frowned. "No, I suppose it doesn't."

"Brittany," Jake said, giving her his most quizzical lifted-eyebrow look, "do you always give name, rank, and team position when you introduce people? Has the Geneva Convention been extended to include ball players?"

The comment sparked a round of nervous laughter from everyone. It was enough to break the ice.

Fred thrust out his hand toward Jake and grinned. "You thought we were carrying Brittany off for the proverbial fate worse than death, did you?"

"You *were*, as far as I'm concerned," Brittany said, then turned to Jake. "These . . . these *nitwits* . . . stalked me along the seawall. They knew the timing of my morning walks here, so they took up jogging to run me down. Can you believe it?"

Their scheme was planned better than his, Jake thought, but it was similar enough that he didn't meet Brittany's gaze directly as he mumbled, "It certainly does seem like extreme behavior."

After nodding and looking away, Brittany glanced sharply back at Jake, noticing that his expression was oddly self-conscious. An idea popped into her mind, but she rejected it. Jake knew where she lived, and he certainly could get in touch with her at work, so why would he go to the trouble of tracking her down during her morning walk?

"Just what was this fate worse than death, if not the usual one?" Jake asked in an effort to divert Brittany's thoughts.

Brittany glowered with mock disgust at the other two men. "Larry and Fred have been bugging me to play shortstop for the Hotshots, and they won't listen when I tell them I'm not interested in adding any more Least Valuable Player awards to my collection. So they decided to hijack me and hold me hostage until I promised to show up at tonight's game."

"Don't make it sound so criminal," Fred protested. "We just wanted to keep you in one place long enough to get you to listen to us."

Great minds do think alike, Jake mused, suppressing a guilty smile. *Or frustrated ones.*

"Britt, we keep trying to tell you it doesn't matter how lousy a player you are," Larry said. "This pickup league of ours is strictly for fun."

"Oh, sure. I've seen some of those games. I've heard the catcalls when somebody misses a fly ball or strikes out. Forget it, boys. And if you keep bugging me, I'll . . ." She turned to Jake with a wink. "I'll hand you over to my bodyguard."

Jake managed a casual grin, but Brittany's playful words made his heart sing. He didn't feel quite so idiotic about having reacted as if he were in a war zone.

"C'mon, Britt," Larry coaxed. "The season's just starting, and if we can't get enough people together for tonight's game, word will start getting around that the Hotshots pull no-shows. What self-respecting team will book with us then?"

"Larry, are you trying to tell me you can't find nine

people from all the hotels in the West End?" Brittany said with undisguised disbelief. "Nine people?"

"It's true! There are too many conventions going on at the big hotels this week, Britt. People who aren't putting in overtime tonight are resting up from the extra hours they've already worked. So be a sport, will you?" Larry coaxed doggedly. "We'll all cover for you in the field. And if anybody tries booing you for striking out or missing a catch . . ." He grinned at Jake. "There's always your personal Lethal Weapon here to discourage rudeness."

Brittany regarded Jake with sudden conjecture. "Did your military-brat upbringing include ball diamonds?"

"Of course," Jake answered carefully, realizing he was about to be roped into playing. He wouldn't mind, as long as Brittany didn't expect him to fill her spot on the team while she made other plans. "Can you imagine a little bit of America anywhere that didn't include our national game?"

"And did you play much of your national game?"

"Some. Not slo-pitch, though."

"Close enough," she said firmly. "Since you're a long-term Somerset resident, it's legitimate for you to be a Hotshot. What do you say, Jake? Would you consider giving the gang a hand tonight?"

"Depends," Jake answered, his gaze locked on hers as he decided to turn the situation to his advantage.

"On what?" Brittany asked with a sudden catch in her voice. Dark flames in Jake's eyes made her senses reel.

"I'll play on one condition," he said quietly.

"Name it!" Fred urged.

Jake gave Brittany a slow, challenging smile. "The

shortstop I'm replacing shows up in the cheering section."

"Done!" Larry said, grabbing Jake's hand and pumping it vigorously.

Still mesmerized by Jake's eyes, Brittany didn't react for a moment. Then, as she realized that Larry had answered for her, she shook herself out of her trance and scowled at him. "Do I get a say in this?"

All three men smiled at her—Jake with wicked satisfaction, Larry and Fred with teeth-baring menace.

Brittany's eyes widened to enormous proportions. She thought things over for three seconds, then nodded with exaggerated enthusiasm. "I can do that," she said agreeably. "I can show up and cheer for the Hotshots. You bet, fellas. I'll be there. That's a lock."

After the others had left the scene, an awkward silence descended between Jake and Brittany. They looked everywhere but at each other, neither of them coming up with a word to say.

The instant she'd been left without the comic relief of Larry and Fred, Brittany remembered her panicky flight from Jake in the hotel lobby the previous afternoon. She was afraid he would ask her why she'd bolted, and she had no idea how to explain. What could she say? That when she'd looked up and spotted him across the room, the poignant tenderness in his eyes had caught her off guard and brought her to the edge of tears? That if she hadn't streaked upstairs to her office, she'd have run straight into his arms, telling him—and anyone else who cared to listen—that she would take whatever crumbs of time and emotion he could spare for her?

What if she'd been mistaken? What if she'd read more into his expression than had been there?

Remembering the apple she still had in her backpack, she decided to dig it out, if only for something to do until the conversation started.

Jake watched as Brittany struggled to get at the nylon sack. She'd done it so easily a few minutes before, he was surprised when she finally heaved a frustrated sigh, slid the straps off her shoulders, and plunked the bag on the ground. As she dropped to a crouch and started fumbling with the buckle, he saw that her fingers were trembling. He couldn't help being glad she was as unnerved as he was.

It occurred to him that Brittany inspired strange lapses in his mental processes—especially in his ability to think things through. With the same lack of foresight that had made him decide to pursue her without any consideration for the long-term future, and with the same tunnel vision that had made him attack her friends first and ask questions later, he'd been so hell-bent on meeting her during a seawall stroll, he hadn't figured out what to say to her once they were alone. If he were to approach his work the same way, he mused, he'd have to turn in his hard hat and slide rule.

When he noticed himself actually scuffing his toe on the ground like a bashful adolescent, an involuntary chuckle escaped him.

Brittany frowned as she straightened up, apple in hand, shrugging her backpack into place again. She wished she could get over the silly, tongue-tied shyness that afflicted her every time she was near Jake. For a passing moment she wondered if he was amused by his effect on her.

Jake saw her expression and said hastily, "I'm still feeling like a bit of an ass for flying off the handle the way I did with your would-be abductors. I guess I'm having trouble getting used to normal civilization, to being in a place where people can kid about such things and pull them as pranks."

Brittany told herself she should have known Jake was more likely to laugh at himself than at her. "I thought we agreed you weren't supposed to apologize," she said firmly.

True, Jake thought as he smiled down at her. But he hadn't been able to think of anything else to say. In any case the silence was broken at last. He'd reached the point where reciting the alphabet had started to seem like a good idea.

Brittany returned his smile, then held out the apple. "Would you like a bite?" she offered. "Or, if you happen to be carrying a jackknife, we could share."

Jake's lips twitched, and his brows performed their amused little quirk.

Brittany looked at him, then at the apple, and barely managed to suppress a groan as she twigged to the Adam-and-Eve symbolism of her offer.

Without comment Jake took the apple and cupped it in one palm, then closed his other hand over it and twisted as if removing a stubborn jar cap.

Brittany swallowed hard as the apple split cleanly in two. "Gulp," she said with exaggerated horror. "Larry and Fred have no idea how lucky they are. By the way, I hope you won't mind if you take a ribbing tonight. A lot of kidding around goes on at the games, and those two clowns might decide to tell everybody about their narrow escape."

Jake handed her one of the halves. "I won't mind, Brittany. I'm looking forward to the evening."

Brittany bit into the crisp fruit and munched thoughtfully as she looked out toward the gently rolling waters of the Pacific, thinking about all the places Jake must have been, the hair-raising adventures he'd survived. "You're a good sport, Jake. A pickup ball game in a Vancouver schoolyard can't be your idea of an exciting time."

"I've had all I need of excitement for the time being," he said quietly.

For the time being, Brittany repeated silently, a familiar knot of sadness forming inside her. *But for how long?*

Another silence fell, broken only by the whooshing of waves washing over the rock-studded beach below the seawall and the raucous cries of quarreling gulls.

Brittany bent down to scoop up a pebble. Straightening up, she threw the small rock so that it arced over the beach and landed in the water with a firm plop and a flurry of ripples. "What's out there, Jake?" she asked softly. "I'm such a homebody, I haven't gone very far or to very many places. What have I been missing?"

"I've started wondering the same thing about myself," he said.

Brittany looked up at him with a quizzical smile. "You? There can't be much you've missed."

"You'd be surprised," he said. "For that matter *I* might be surprised." Deciding they were getting too serious, he grinned. "One thing I know I've been missing is a pickup ball game in a schoolyard with a pretty cheerleader on the sidelines rooting for me." Glancing to the right and left of him, he said out of the side of his mouth, "Now, do you think maybe I should tag along for the rest of your morning stroll just in case the Surrey lacrosse team is lurking in the bushes to commandeer you?"

Taken aback, Brittany burst out laughing. "Good idea. And since my bodyguard is with me, maybe we could cut through the park. I love the smell of fresh cedar when it's still damp with morning dew, but I tend to keep to the seawall when I'm on my own."

"I gather Casey still isn't well enough to join you," Jake said as they fell in step beside each other, heading into the lush regions of the forest preserve.

"No, she isn't. The poor thing's really . . ." Brittany's words trailed off, and she gave Jake a puzzled frown. "I don't remember mentioning Casey's morning sickness to you. I don't remember mentioning Casey at all."

"You didn't. Helena did."

Brittany stopped in her tracks. "Helena? Helena Danforth told you about my best friend's morning sickness?"

Jake nodded, smiling. "So I went to Chinatown, found a good herbalist, and got him to blend a couple of teas that might help Casey. I'll drop them off at your office later today if you'd like to give them to her to try. I'll include the recipes so that she can check them out with her doctor, though they're just mixtures of ordinary ingredients, such as peppermint and chamomile, raspberry leaf and lemon balm—that sort of thing."

Brittany stared at him in astonishment. "How would you know about teas to alleviate morning sickness?"

"Actually they're good for any nausea, and I know about them because collecting folk medicine is a hobby of mine. I'm fascinated by the natural cures people in different cultures have come up with for everyday miseries, especially in areas where conventional medical facilities leave a lot to be desired."

Suddenly aware how little she really knew about Jake Mallory, Brittany wondered again how she could be drawn so powerfully to someone who was such a stranger to her.

Then she recalled the speech she'd made to Jake about her need for a sense of community, for "connectedness" with other people, and she winced with a new rush of embarrassment. The next time she was thinking of launching into that kind of lecture, she vowed, she would learn something about her listener before she opened her mouth. Jake had been in town for less than a week, yet already he'd carved out a special niche for himself. "You went to all that trouble for Casey?" she said, still astounded. "For someone you haven't even met?"

Jake shrugged. "Why not? Do you know that old man you tossed your other apple to a little while ago?"

"You saw that exchange?" Beginning to wonder if anything ever got past Jake, Brittany shook her head and laughed. "That situation's different. It's a ritual that started by accident. During one of my walks a couple weeks ago I was about to bite into a juicy Okanagan apple when I saw that sweet old man staring at it like a kid pressing his nose against a candy-store window. What could I do? I gave him the apple. The next day I took two along—one for him and one for me. It's gotten to be a habit. But you went out of your way . . ."

"I heard that a friend of yours wasn't feeling well," Jake cut in, "and thought perhaps I could help. It's no big deal."

Rolling her eyes, Brittany said, "According to you, being taken hostage in the Middle East wasn't a big deal."

"Compared with some of the horrors I saw other

people endure over there, it wasn't," Jake said matter-of-factly, then held out his hand to her. "Now, are we going to walk or not?"

Brittany instinctively put her hand in his, and currents of warmth and electricity sang through her. His touch was like his gaze, she mused. Mesmerizing, exciting, and unbearably erotic.

They'd walked for several minutes before Brittany suddenly gave Jake a puzzled look, cocking her head to one side. "Jake, weren't you going the opposite way before you met up with me?" she asked.

"I was," he admitted, giving her hand a gentle squeeze. "But for you, Brittany, I'll gladly switch directions."

Brittany smiled as if taking his comment at face value, but she wondered if he was talking about more than a walk on the Stanley Park seawall.

Dressed for slo-pitch success in jeans and the green-and-white Hotshots jersey that had been delivered to his suite along with a fielder's glove during the afternoon, Jake was parking his car in front of Brittany's apartment building when she burst through the wide doorway as if she'd stepped on an Eject button in the lobby.

As he hopped out of the car and went around to the passenger side to open the door and help her with the large club bag she was carrying, Jake chuckled. Brittany's whole look underscored her enthusiasm and sense of fun. Her hair was in its jaunty topknot again, secured with a white terry-cloth band and bouncing perkily. She was wearing white shorts, a bright green T-shirt cropped at the waist, and matching green sneakers—the colors obviously chosen to identify her with the Hotshots.

She made Jake want to bundle her onto a south-bound jet and spirit her off to his place in Santa Barbara, where he could have her all to himself. Her natural appeal excited him beyond anything he'd ever experienced before. The cool beauties he'd gravitated to in the past seemed boring by comparison. "Hi, gorgeous," he said with a wink, trying his best not to come across like the wolf meeting Red Riding Hood on her way to Granny's.

"Hi," Brittany answered softly. Jake's predatory expression, veiled so quickly by his cavalier wink, triggered an answering hunger in her. As he took the club bag and tossed it into the backseat, she watched the easy male grace of his movements and the ripple of muscle under his shirt, sorely tempted to entice him up to her apartment and let the Hotshots fend for themselves.

But she sighed, gave Jake a shy smile, and climbed into the car.

"Why does a one-woman cheering section need a club bag big enough for a pro-hockey player?" Jake asked when he was behind the wheel.

"Don't be silly. You couldn't fit a pro-hockey player into that thing," she retorted, not ready to tell him what was in the bag.

Chuckling, Jake impulsively leaned over to touch his lips to her cheek. He knew he'd made a mistake as he breathed in the scent of strawberries mingled with spring flowers and felt the softness of her skin. She was delicious, and his craving for her was insatiable.

But he remembered what he'd told himself just before leaving the hotel a few minutes before: Only the strongest foundations were worth building on, and strong foundations took time to put in place.

Reluctantly drawing away from Brittany, Jake managed to focus his attention on driving to the schoolyard on the far side of English Bay for a slo-pitch game that seemed a poor substitute for what he had in mind.

Six

When they reached the playing field, Brittany chose a spot to one side of the backstop, well back of the first-base line. There were no bleachers, so she took a tiny folding seat from her club bag and placed it at a vantage point for watching all the action.

After introducing Jake to the players from both teams and agreeing to join them at a West End pub for a postgame beer, Brittany drew Jake aside. With a mischievous grin, she reached into the bag again, pulled out two green-and-white pom-poms, and shook them as she did a little prance back in forth in front of him, chanting so that only he could hear, "Give us an *M*! Give us an *A*! Give us an *L-L-O-R-Y*! Mallory! Mallory! That's our guy!"

Jake tipped back his head and roared with laughter.

"You want a cheerleader," Brittany said with a lift of her chin, "you get a cheerleader."

"Oh, I want a cheerleader," he said with sudden seductiveness. "One cheerleader in particular."

Brittany's pulse thrummed wildly, and her laugh was shaky. "I'll bet you say that to all the—"

"Play ball!" the umpire shouted.

Saved by the call, Brittany thought. "Okay, Hot-shot," she said to Jake with a playful bravado she didn't feel, "it's rah-rah-sis-boom-bah time. Get out there and give it everything you've got."

She was nervous when he was up for his first time at bat: she wanted him to do well because she was responsible for getting him involved in the game. Her heart sank when the first strike slipped by him, then the second. He seemed to be having trouble getting used to the slow, lobbing pitch.

But as the ball crossed the plate for the third time, Jake connected hard and straight for an easy triple, and from then on he showed no mercy.

By the end of the third inning Brittany knew that nobody was likely to kid Jake about the seawall incident or anything else. He was shaping up to be the Hotshots' secret weapon—one they needed badly against a far superior team.

Although she'd started out to play cheerleader as a joke, Brittany found herself shaking her pom-poms with the fervor of a college coed, shouting lustily and jumping up and down with uninhibited glee every time Jake's bat hammered the ball.

The Hotshots were out in the field and Brittany was perched on her folding chair when she noticed an attractive redhead ride up on a bicycle, lean it against the rear of the backstop, then saunter to the sidelines where she stood watching the game for a few minutes, her hands shoved into the back pockets of her jeans.

When the game's umpire, a young man who looked like a fraternal twin of the new arrival, caught the redhead's eye and waved, she nodded curtly and plunked down cross-legged on the grass near Brittany.

Brittany returned her attention to the game. To Jake specifically. She loved watching his fluid movements and relaxed expertise. He was fast and strong and sleek, a natural athlete in command of his body, and Brittany couldn't help dwelling on the pleasures that body could offer a woman. Heat spiraled through her like liquid smoke. Her mouth went dry, and her palms felt damp as sensual images began dominating her mind.

She willed herself to pay attention to the action on the field.

By the bottom of the fourth inning the Hotshots had taken a narrow lead. Brittany was caught up in the tension of the close game, jumping to her feet and rooting for her team as if it were within a hair's breadth of winning the World Series.

It was Jake's turn at bat again. As he strode toward the plate, Brittany cupped her hands at the sides of her mouth and hollered, "Yay, Jake! Give us another grand slam homer!"

He glanced over his shoulder at her, chuckled, and shook his head, then gave her a casual little two-finger salute and positioned himself with a provocative shifting of his hips.

"He can't hit a grand slam," the redhead piped up.

"Jake can do anything," Brittany said without taking her eyes off him.

He didn't let her down; he hit the ball out of the park.

"It's not a grand slam," Brittany heard after she'd stopped jumping up and down and cheering. "The bases have to be loaded for a homer to be called a grand slam."

Brittany turned to the redhead. "Excuse me?"

"Loaded, meaning a runner on each base. There

was nobody on, so it's not a grand slam. Don't you know anything about this game?"

"I know how to enjoy it," Brittany said with a smile, determined not to let anyone spoil her fun. "Why are you here if you're so unhappy about it? You don't seem to be having a good time, and you certainly aren't trying to make friends." She walked over to the other woman and thrust out her hand. "So why not start with me? I'm Britt Thomas, and I'm doing my cheerleader number rather than make an even worse fool of myself trying to play ball."

The other woman grudgingly reached up to accept the proffered handshake. "Karen Blackwell. I'm taking over from my brother as umpire in a few minutes because he has to leave early. I owe him a favor, or I wouldn't waste my time. I don't know why you people want an umpire anyway. In this pickup league nobody knows or cares about the rules. Why anyone bothers coming out for the games is beyond me."

"For the fun of it," Brittany said cheerfully. "I don't think the whole thing's meant to be taken too seriously."

Karen rolled her eyes. "This from a pom-pom girl?"

Brittany laughed. "You do have a point there," she admitted.

"Karen, can you take over now?" the umpire yelled.

Karen uncrossed her legs, stood up, and strolled over to take her brother's place behind the plate.

The league's games were seven innings long. The Hotshots had fallen behind by two runs, and it was their last turn at bat in the bottom of the seventh.

The score hadn't changed when it was Jake's turn at the plate, and Brittany couldn't understand how he could look so calm when he was on the spot.

There were two outs and three players on base. He could be the hero or the goat, and Brittany's heart pounded as if he were a Roman gladiator whose very life depended on the outcome of the contest.

"Another homer, Jake!" she shouted. Grinning as she saw Karen glancing over at her, Brittany added, "The bases are loaded, baby, so give us the old grand slam!"

Obligingly Jake did just that on the very first pitch.

Brittany was beside herself with excitement as the third Hotshot crossed the plate for the winning run, and by the time Jake reached home, she was catapulting toward him, hurling herself into his arms and laughing exultantly.

"You're terrific!" she cried as his big hands circled her waist and he grinned up at her. Still hanging on to her pom-poms, she wrapped her arms around his neck and her legs around his lean hips. "You're fabulous! You're the all-time Hotshot Hero!"

"And you, Kitten," he said in a low rasp, "are the most inspiring cheering section a man ever had."

His sultry tone, effortless strength, and radiant warmth made Brittany's whole body soften like a popsicle on a hot day. The ball field and all the people on it faded into a blurred background, the cheering muffled by the blood roaring in her ears. "Jake," she whispered. "Oh, Jake, I . . ."

"He may be a Hotshot hero to you," she heard a familiar voice drawl, cutting through her sensual daze, "but I say the man's out."

Brittany blinked slowly, realizing that her nemesis was trying to have the last laugh by resorting to spite. "What did you say?" she asked as she turned and looked over her shoulder at Karen Blackwell.

"You heard me. Your hero's out."

"How can you say that?" Brittany demanded,

clambering off Jake and hitting the ground in a hands-on-hips, feet-astride, chin-thrusting stance. "You know perfectly well that Jake made it home before the fielder even got his hands on the ball!"

The sullen umpire looked down her nose at Brittany. "Thanks to you and your flying leap onto him, Mr. Grand Slam didn't touch the plate, little girl. The catcher, however, touched *him*, right after the left fielder threw the ball home. So Big Jake's out, the game's over, and I finally get to blow this pop stand." After pivoting on her heel, Karen began striding toward her car.

Brittany's frayed patience snapped. She tore after Karen, grabbed her arm, and whirled her around, standing on tiptoe so that they were more or less nose-to-nose. "Jake *did* touch home plate! He wouldn't make a mistake like that, even if I distracted him. He just wouldn't! I don't know what your problem is, lady, but—"

"Honey," Jake cut in, "it's all right. The Hotshots won anyway."

"No, it is *not* all right," Brittany insisted without looking back at him. "This . . . this *grouch* isn't going to get away with saying you were out when you weren't!"

"Read my lips," Karen said with exaggerated patience. "He's out. I made the call and I'm sticking with it, understand? Now, take your pom-poms and go home to your Malibu Barbie dolls like a good girl, okay?"

Brittany threw down the shakers and narrowed her eyes as she curled her hands into fists and reared back. "Why, you . . . I'll . . . I'll pom-pom *you*, you—"

Suddenly she felt herself leaving the ground, lifted

onto Jake's hip and held there by one of his powerful
arms while Karen smirked and walked away.

"What are you doing?" Brittany cried, pummeling
the air. "Put me down, Jake Mallory!"

Ignoring her orders, Jake asked someone to return
her pom-poms and folding chair to her club bag.

Brittany grumbled and pushed at Jake's arm in
vain while her things were gathered up and the bag
handed to him; but when Larry chortled as Jake
started ambling off the field with her still perched on
his hip, she erupted. "You think this is funny, Larry
Armstrong? Twice now in one day I've been as-
saulted by male gorillas, this time by the very gorilla
I was defending against rank injustice, and you get a
big kick out of it? Well, I fail to see the humor, thank
you very much!"

Everyone else on both teams saw a great deal of
humor, however, and their approving laughter and
applause reverberated in Brittany's ears all the way
to Jake's car.

He managed to open the passenger door without
putting her down. After carefully depositing her on
the passenger seat, he strode around to the driver's
side while Brittany folded her arms over her chest
and scowled, facing straight ahead. She realized that
she might have seen the comedy of the situation
more readily if her body weren't crackling with erotic
energy, but she wasn't about to admit it. She didn't
want to be amused or aroused, and she refused to be
turned on by the second glimpse she was getting in
one day of an unpredictable, volatile, perhaps even
dangerous Jake Mallory. She simply would not be
that kind of idiotic female!

"Let me make something crystal clear," she began
the instant Jake was behind the wheel. "It's one
thing for you to act first and ask questions later in a

situation that appears threatening, but this kind of macho posturing is another matter entirely! I don't care if it goes over big in Australia or Arabia or wherever else you've been hanging your hard hat lately. I won't put up with it, understand? I will not allow—"

She stopped abruptly as Jake turned to her with an enigmatic smile and a blazing intensity in his eyes that made her throat close over.

"Are you talking about my macho posturing?" he said softly. "Or yours?"

The comment brought Brittany sharply to her senses. He was right, she realized. *She* was the one who'd turned into Rah-Rah-Rambo. What had got into her?

A tiny giggle escaped her constricted throat but died after one tremulous trill, squelched by the unprecedented aura of purpose in Jake's manner. The very air around him suddenly seemed so galvanized, she half believed she would be zapped if she ventured too close . . . yet she was drawn to him as helplessly as an iron filing to an electromagnetic force.

Jake started the car and negotiated it from its tight parking spot.

Several minutes passed without another word from him. Brittany, too, remained silent, her thoughts tumbling over one another as she wondered what was going through Jake's mind.

Eventually she began to wonder if he was angry with her for the ridiculous scene she'd made. She was upset at herself, for that matter. And the more she thought about her foolish tantrum, the more disturbed she became. It was bad enough she'd lost her temper over a stupid ball game when she'd never done such a ridiculous thing before in her life, but to have lost her head in front of Jake was doubly humiliating. She doubted very much that her sophisticated rivals would indulge in such childish behavior.

Brittany swallowed hard. *Rivals.* Oh, Lord. The truth was out. Other women were competition. She wanted to win Jake for herself. Permanently. All her running away had been for nothing—a sour-grapes ploy to shield herself from the pain of ultimately losing him.

Well, this time she'd wrecked her chances with Jake once and for all. She could see his disgust in the hard line of his mouth and the rigidity of his body as he kept his hands curled tightly around the steering wheel and his eyes on the traffic ahead. He was so steamed, his mind seemed to be wandering. He missed the turn to get to the pub. "You've overshot the street we wanted," she told him in a small, strained voice.

"I know," he answered. A moment later he wheeled onto Brittany's street.

Her eyes widened. Was he taking her straight home? "We promised to meet the others," she reminded.

"I know," Jake answered again.

"Well, naturally you can do whatever you like, but I intend to keep that . . ." Brittany's voice trailed off as Jake drove past her apartment building.

Clamping her lips together, she decided to wait and see what the man was planning before she uttered another sound.

He headed into Stanley Park, taking several little-used roads until they'd reached a secluded area somewhere in the middle of the sprawling forest preserve.

Brittany was dumbfounded. Did Jake feel he

needed even more privacy than her apartment offered so that he could give full vent to his anger?

Jake pulled the car to the side of the road, switched off the ignition, and got out to stride around to the passenger side. Opening the door with one hand, he held out the other to Brittany.

"This place doesn't look like a pub to me," she said, folding her hands in her lap.

Jake reached into the car, wrapped his fingers around her wrist, and tugged gently but firmly.

Brittany got the message. He wasn't about to take no for an answer.

She climbed out of the car and let Jake lead her along a narrow footpath to an even more sheltered spot amid giant evergreens, tall birches, and lush ferns. The air was sultry, rich with the scent of musk and cedar and pine, unreached by an ocean breeze. The silence seemed infinite, the forest cover impenetrable, offering only a glimpse of sky through the unremitting green of the dense foliage overhead. Brittany felt as if she'd stepped into another time and place, primeval and dizzying in its raw sensuality.

Jake stopped at last and curved his fingers around Brittany's upper arms, turning her to face him. "What the devil am I going to do with you?" he demanded.

"Who's asking you to do anything?" Brittany retorted, blinking back treacherous tears.

He hauled her against him and lowered his mouth over hers in a fiercely passionate kiss. When he raised his head moments later, Brittany stared up at him in confusion.

"You're driving me crazy," Jake growled. "Every damn time I think I have control of myself, you do something that knocks the pins out from under me.

Why did you leap to my defense over an umpire's bad call in a pickup game, Brittany? Why?"

She tried to twist out of his arms, but his hold was too tight. "All right, so I made a fool of myself," she admitted, glad to get the subject out into the open. "I lost my head and acted like a bad-tempered brat. You're shocked. You're appalled. Okay, I don't blame you. I apologize if you were embarrassed."

"I'm shocked, yes. But appalled? Embarrassed? Not on your life, sweetheart. And keep your apology. Just answer my question. Why did you do it?"

"I have no idea! It just happened!"

"No it didn't," Jake shot back. "I'll tell you why you got so hot under the collar."

She blinked slowly, all at once becoming wary. '*You'll* tell me? You know something I don't?"

"I know this much, honey. You blew it tonight. You really blew it."

She caught her breath as if he'd struck her. To her horror she felt two tears spilling from her eyes. 'Okay, I blew it. I didn't know my fall from grace was all that serious, but if you think it was, that's your privilege."

Jake's brows drew together in sudden puzzlement. 'What do you mean? More to the point, what do you think *I* meant?"

It struck Brittany that she might have misinterpreted Jake's comment. For him to suggest she'd lost him with her display was out of character. He wasn't that egotistical. "What *did* you mean?" she asked with a sniff.

Jake heaved an exasperated sigh. "Would it be possible, just once, for you to give me a straight answer instead of parrying with another question?"

"Would it be possible for *you* to come up with a straight answer?" Brittany said in a small voice, once more trying to wriggle away from him but meeting with the same lack of success. She sniffed again. "Anyway, by now I haven't the faintest idea what we're talking about."

Reaching up to cradle her face between his palms, Jake gently brushed away her tears with the sides of his thumbs. "We're talking," he said in measured syllables, "about how you blew your cover a little while ago."

"Blew my cover?" Brittany repeated. "What cover?"

"You know what cover."

"Here we go again," Brittany said, trying to sound frustrated despite the amusement suddenly tugging at the corners of her mouth. "If I knew, I wouldn't have to ask, would I?"

"Think about it," Jake suggested with a smile, then dipped his head and recaptured her mouth.

Brittany wondered vaguely how he expected her to think about anything when his lips were moving over hers, his tongue thrusting into the recesses of her mouth, his hands drifting down her body to explore its contours.

"Have you figured it out yet?" he said, still kissing her as he spoke, his breath hot and sweet.

Brittany hadn't figured out anything but that she liked the form Jake's anger seemed to be taking. She was tempted to goad him into an all-out rage just to see what delicious sensations he would dole out as punishment.

Pushing her hands up under his jersey, she glided her palms over the solid breadth of his chest, re-learning its hard planes, its tautness, its textures.

Jake let out a quiet groan. One of his hands slid downward to the base of her spine, the fingers splayed and digging into her soft flesh, while the other slipped under her shirt, deftly found and undid the front hook of her bra, and began stroking her breasts. It was Brittany's turn to moan with pleasure, and Jake took the sound into his mouth as his lips closed again over hers.

It was late in the evening. Even the midsummer sun would have to set very soon, and the few shards of light piercing the leafy forest ceiling would be extinguished. "We could make love right here," she murmured.

"We could," Jake agreed. He nibbled at her lower lip until it was swollen and pink, then soothed it with his tongue while his fingers teased the peaks of her breasts to eager attention. "We shouldn't of course."

"Of course," Brittany said in a breathless whisper. "I mean . . . well, you never know when some happy camper will come yodeling down the trail, even when it's an obscure path in the farthest reaches of the park."

He chuckled quietly and sprinkled light kisses over her cheeks and temples and eyelids. "Besides, we did promise to meet the others at the pub."

Brittany made feathery circles over his hard male nipples as she grazed her lips along the underside of his jaw. "And it would be rude of us not to show up."

"You're right, sweetheart. We'd better go."

Sighing, she nuzzled into the fragrant warmth of his throat. "Yes, we'd better.

They stood for several minutes more, kissing and caressing each other as if to store up the sweet sensations.

"There's something you should know," Jake said, gently rolling her engorged nipples between thumb and forefinger, making them ache for the moist warmth of his mouth. "The gloves are off now, Brittany."

"Oh, good," she whispered, barely listening as her body responded to his touch. When his words finally registered, she asked raggedly, "What do you mean, the gloves are off?"

He smiled and slid his hands downward to rest lightly on her slender waist. "The kid gloves, sweetheart. Because that's what I've been treating you with. I've been so careful not to pressure you, not to take advantage of your vulnerability. I've analyzed my feelings and your reactions until my head's spinning. That foolishness is over, Brittany. From now on I go with what I feel and what I know. We'll leave here and spend a little while socializing at the pub like good sports, but afterward it'll be—pardon the pun—a whole new ball game."

Brittany thrilled to his words and his certainty, his voice itself triggering vibrations of erotic excitement deep within her. "What brought about this change of heart?" she asked huskily.

"You did," he answered. "You, my little pom-pom-wielding sidekick, with your streak of fierce protectiveness. I'm a self-reliant man. Always have been. I was brought up that way. I'm not used to having anyone leap to my defense."

"Especially over such a trivial matter," Brittany put in with a sheepish, shaky laugh.

"Exactly. So it boggles the mind to think what you'd be like in a serious situation." Jake crooked his index finger under her chin. "I wanted us to put down a foundation we could build on, but tonight I saw in a flash that the foundation's already there. It's been there all along. I said I'd wait until you were ready to go all the way with me when we make love, no regrets afterward. But you're ready, Brittany. You're there. The doubts are gone."

Brittany stared up at him, finally understanding what her outburst at the ballpark had revealed.

A silvery twinkle appeared in Jake's eyes as he put her thoughts into words. "In your own inimitable way, sweetheart, you gave notice that hassling Jake Mallory means tangling with you. You told me and everyone else on the scene how much I matter to you." Brushing the backs of his fingers over Brittany's cheek, he added softly, "I couldn't go straight from the game to the bar at that point, and I couldn't tell you what I was feeling because I was . . . well . . . a trifle overcome."

A trifle overcome, Brittany thought, her eyes filling with tears again. Coming from a rough-hewn man of action like Jake, the words were lyric poetry.

"Let's get out of here," he said with unexpected gruffness, draping an arm over Brittany's shoulder to steer her back to the car.

Brittany held back. In the midst of the scented glade she felt so close to Jake, so right in his arms. Everything seemed so simple. "I hate to leave," she murmured. "There's magic for us here, Jake."

Jake understood her reluctance to go. He felt the same way. But he smiled and urged Brittany forward. "There's magic for us everywhere," he said quietly. "You'll see."

Seven

Letting his eyes adjust to the dim lighting, Jake stood with Brittany just inside the door of the pub, his hand resting on the small of her back. He couldn't seem to get enough of touching her. Any excuse would do. Or no excuse. All he really needed was the opportunity.

He scanned the place with a practiced eye and saw that it was nothing fancy, just a bare-bones North American watering hole, the tables small, square, and orange-Formica-topped, the captain's chairs dark wood with brown vinyl seats, the hardwood floor in need of a sanding and polishing.

Not exactly romantic, Jake mused, lightly grazing his fingers up and down Brittany's spine. But he was confident that the sparks between them would be ignited in any setting, even a raucous beer joint.

"There's our group," he said when he spotted several teammates in a far corner. "Shall we join them and get the where-have-you-been questions over with?"

Brittany smiled up at him. "Ready if you are,

Champ." Her offhand banter belied the flutters in the pit of her stomach. It wasn't the prospect of being teased by the others about their temporary disappearing act that unnerved her. It was Jake's habit of maintaining almost constant physical contact with her, sending quivers of excitement through her body. She wondered if he could feel the tremors, the electricity and heat he generated in her whole being with only a casual caress.

He pressed his palm against her back to propel her toward the section of the pub where several tables had been pushed together to form two long ones.

Jake noted one problem. There were spare chairs, but not two together. He had no intention of sitting apart from Brittany, so he decided a little body language was in order. As soon as he and Brittany reached one of the tables, he moved his hand to the back of her neck, a proprietary signal meant to get his message across.

As he saw that the members of the opposing teams were sitting together at random—the rivalry on the ball field having given way to the easy camaraderie of longtime friends—Jake decided he liked the atmosphere even if it didn't lend itself to a subtle seduction. The waiters knew some of their customers by name, kept the moisture-beaded beer jugs filled without being asked, and traded quips as they collected their tabs from bills tossed onto the middle of the table. At least five conversations were going on at once, some a low hum from two or three people, others lively shouting matches from table to table.

Simple rituals, Jake thought. They provided continuity. A sense of belonging. Such things were very important to Brittany. Could they become as important to him?

Perhaps. He'd never have thought so before, but all at once anything seemed possible.

"Hey, we were about to give up on you two," Larry Armstrong said as Jake and Brittany reached the tables. "Where'd you . . . ?" His question ended abruptly as his wife elbowed him in the ribs, smiling innocently. He turned and gave her a puzzled look, then shrugged and pushed back his chair, getting to his feet. "Let's make room here, guys. Musical-chairs time. Everybody move down a couple of seats."

Jake grinned as he and Brittany crowded into two vacated chairs beside each other. He was beginning to like her friends very much. They were as quick as certain Aussies to pick up on signals.

As he reached into his pocket for his wallet to add a few bills to the pot, Brittany opened her purse to do the same. Jake closed his hand around hers. "I'll take care of your share," he said firmly.

"That's not the way things are done around here," Brittany protested, amazed that even the most innocent contact with Jake made her tingle from head to toe. "We women pay our own way."

"What about couples?" he asked with a lift of his brows. "Larry and his wife, for instance."

"Well . . . that's different, of course. . . ."

"I'll take care of your share," Jake repeated, his gaze locking on Brittany's.

Another thrill raced through her as she realized he was stating that she was now part of a couple.

He proceeded to drive the point home with subtly possessive gestures—draping his arm over the back of her chair and idly caressing the curve of her shoulder, pouring her beer and letting his fingers brush hers as he handed her the glass, leaning down so that his lips were close to her ear when he asked her to jog his memory with a name he'd forgotten. He was being attentive and charming. He was letting it be known that she was his. And Brittany loved every minute of it.

Jake was halfway through his second beer when Brittany, still nursing her first, realized that he'd been quiet for a while, a faraway look in his eyes. Instantly her deep insecurities shot to the surface. Was the magic fading for him already? Now that he knew he'd won her, was he losing interest in the chase? Was he bored with the pub and her friends? With the triteness of it all? "Penny for your thoughts?" she said, wincing inwardly as soon as she'd spoken. Even her question was a cliché.

"Oh, I was just getting a kick out of this scene," Jake hedged, preferring to save his actual thoughts for later. They were definitely X-rated.

"You're not bored, then?"

Jake smiled and reached up to brush back a few stray tendrils of chestnut hair from Brittany's cheek. "How could I be bored, sweetheart? I'm with you."

Brittany's heart skipped several beats. She wanted to be satisfied with Jake's reassurance, but some gremlin inside her had to push. "This kind of evening isn't very glamorous," she said, glancing around the tawdry room.

"What makes you think I care about glamour?"

"I guess I meant exciting," she amended after chewing on her lower lip for a moment. "This must all seem so tame to you."

"Tame," he murmured. As he watched Brittany worry at the full, inviting lip he was longing to nibble on, tameness was an alien concept. The woman was driving him wild. "Doesn't it occur to you," he went on with an effort, "that so-called tame pleasures might appeal to me?"

"For a while, maybe. But not for long. A lone wolf doesn't turn into a domesticated spaniel just because he needs to stop and lick a few wounds."

"You think that's what I'm doing? Licking my wounds?"

Brittany shrugged, wishing she could stop testing the strength of her bond with Jake. Yet she kept right on doing it. "It seems like a logical assumption. You went through a terrible time not very long ago. It can't be easy to keep things in perspective after something as shattering as being held hostage in a foreign country."

"On the contrary, I think the experience helped me *put* things in perspective." Jake realized that there was no point arguing with Brittany about this particular question. Talk was cheap. He grinned instead and made light of the issue. "In any case, there's been nothing tame about this evening. These people are your friends, so it might surprise you to know that when I was standing at home plate for the first time tonight, I looked out at the ball diamond and saw the equivalent of hostile natives, probably questioning my right to trespass on their turf."

He realized he'd gone too far with his teasing when Brittany looked stricken. "Jake, I'm sorry," she said. "I had no idea you might feel out of place. You seem so confident, so at home in any situation. But for the record, nobody on either team questioned your right to be there. Even if some fool had asked how you were connected to the hotel team, I'd have set him straight soon enough. Or her."

"I believe it," Jake drawled, picking up his glass and using it to salute her.

Brittany felt a blush creeping over her cheeks. She clicked glasses with him, then took a healthy swallow of her beer before finally laughing at herself.

"Will I ever live down the fact that I got a little carried away at that game?" She laughed again and added, "Literally!"

"Why don't you try playing for the team sometime?" Jake suggested. "You're probably much better than you think, and nobody could fault your enthusiasm."

"Don't *you* start on me," she said with a grin. "I'm every bit as bad as I think. Maybe worse."

"Didn't you have to play ball at school?"

"Not if I could get out of it. I hid behind the backstop when the teams were being picked. Everyone pretended not to notice."

"The other kids sympathized with your fear of flying softballs?"

"Sympathized? Heavens, no. Neither side wanted to get stuck with me!"

"Maybe I should take you out some afternoon and work on your skills," Jake said, only half jokingly.

"So far you're planning to teach me Japanese and instruct me in the art of self-defense, and now you're talking about being my slow-pitch coach. Are you really such a bear for punishment?"

Jake grinned, looked into her eyes. "A bear for punishment? I was thinking more of the rewards of keeping you after class for special instruction."

Brittany's pulse shot forward, and heat flashed through her like a grass fire in a sudden wind. "I'll bet you could teach me quite a bit," she murmured.

"I'd like to think so," Jake said, his voice deep and intimate. "But you know the old truism about the student teaching the teacher."

Brittany smiled with such warmth, Jake decided it must be time for the pub visit to come to an end.

But all at once her smile faded and turned to a

frown, her attention caught by something over Jake's shoulder.

He turned to follow the direction of her gaze and saw a tall blond man dressed in gray flannel slacks and a navy blazer sauntering toward the table.

Jake looked at Brittany again and knew she didn't like the newcomer. His own hackles went up immediately. If this man had ever hurt her, or bothered her in any way . . .

"Well, if it isn't the late, not-so-great Garth Porter," Larry said, rolling his eyes. "Nice of you to make it *after* the game, big guy. Why did you bug us to put you on the team if you were going to pull a no-show? We'd have been shorthanded if a couple of people hadn't come in at the last minute."

"Sorry," Porter said, flashing a smile that didn't seem at all apologetic. "I got tied up at a dinner meeting that wouldn't quit. How humiliating was tonight's loss?"

"Twelve–eleven," Fred Willoughby answered.

"Thirteen–eleven," Brittany piped up with a quick grin at Jake.

"Thirteen–eleven?" Porter repeated, cocking one pale brow. "Hey, not bad. At least you guys—and gals of course—came in a close second for a change. Sorry I wasn't on hand, but I'll try to make it for the next game."

"Thirteen–eleven for the Hotshots," Fred added with obvious satisfaction.

Porter stared at him. "For the Hotshots? You won?"

"We sure did, Garth baby. You think you can arrange to be tied up at a dinner meeting for our next game?"

Brittany didn't crack up the way several other

onlookers did. Her expression remained impassive, as if she barely acknowledged Porter's existence.

Jake hoped he would never be on the receiving end of her deep freeze.

Obviously not amused by Fred's crack, Porter managed only a tight, phony smile. "Well, congratulations, team. I heard you were going to coax our girl Britt into taking part in the game instead of just watching. Obviously she's a more valuable player than I am."

"Actually it was more a case of Brittany scouting out a more valuable player for us," someone offered.

Porter's glance shifted to Jake, coldly appraising him. "Since you're the only new face around here, I assume you were the ringer of the night. Which hotel do you work for?"

Brittany answered, "Jake's a guest at the Somerset, Garth."

Jake dropped his arm from the back of Brittany's chair and started to get to his feet for a polite handshake with Porter. His inclination was to punch the man in the nose, simply because he thought it might please Brittany, but he figured he'd better not, at least not until he knew a little more about the situation. He didn't want to give her the impression he was a loose cannon careening around in her life.

"Don't get up," Porter said, clamping his hand down on Jake's shoulder.

Jake looked pointedly at the hand. He didn't like that kind of familiarity from strangers.

Garth lifted his hand. "Pleased to meet you, Jake," he said jovially, grabbing a chair from a table behind them and crowding it between Brittany and the person to her left. "I trust you're being well taken care of at our little hostelry?"

Jake frowned. *Our* little hostelry? And earlier, *our*

girl Britt? What did this man have to do with the Somerset? With Brittany?

"Garth's a director on the board of Danforth Developments, the company Helena has been head of since her husband died," Brittany explained. She picked up her glass and drained it, then set it down with a sharp click. "The Somerset isn't part of the corporation, but since it's Helena's, some of the directors seem to take a proprietary interest in it."

Jake nodded, finally understanding Brittany's veneer of politeness. She was trying to be civil to someone Helena had to deal with—but she wasn't having much success. Why did she dislike Porter so intensely? It wasn't like her to be so icy.

Garth poured himself a beer, then leaned forward to peer around Brittany at Jake. "Are you going to be in town long enough to be a regular for the Hotshots, Jake?"

Larry leapt at the suggestion. "Yeah, Jake. How about it?"

"Cool it, Larry," Brittany said. She smiled but spoke as firmly as a parent admonishing an overeager youngster. "Jake isn't in town to rescue floundering slo-pitch teams; he's enjoying some much-needed R and R. He doesn't know how long he'll be here, so there's no sense trying to pin him down."

Jake had the feeling Brittany's warning was as much for her own benefit as for Larry's. "Actually I'll be around for a while," he said as he refilled Brittany's glass from the fresh jug of beer the waiter had plunked down. He smiled at her as he handed her the glass. "I've been offered a short-term contract here, and I've decided to take it."

"A contract?" Brittany said, her eyes suddenly enormous. "In Vancouver?"

Jake nodded. "In Vancouver." He thought Brittany seemed pleased. Taken aback, but pleased.

"What do you do, Jake?" Garth asked, angling his body and draping his arm over the back of Brittany's chair.

She recoiled as if she'd felt a rattler slithering up behind her, and at the same moment saw a dangerous glint appear in Jake's eyes. Springing to her feet, she scraped back her chair, practically dislocating Garth's shoulder in her haste. "While you gentlemen get the lowdown on Jake's profession," she said brightly. "I'm going to go freshen up." Catching Jake's eye, she sent him a pleading look. *No scenes, please!* she urged silently.

He hesitated, his expression unreadable, but finally smiled and gave her a barely perceptible nod.

Brittany turned and hurried to the ladies' room without looking back.

Her mind was in a turmoil. Jake was going to stay in Vancouver for a while. What did "a while" mean? A couple of weeks? A month? Longer?

And what was happening at the table? Was Jake keeping his cool? Was he giving Garth a clear hands-off message? She hoped so. No, she told herself hastily. She didn't hope any such thing. Good grief, she wasn't Jake's possession!

Or was she? Didn't she have to admit she liked his possessiveness? Didn't he make her feel safe, and special, and treasured?

Her lips curved in a smile. Truthfully, wasn't she enjoying the rare luxury of Jake's protective ways, even if he did tend to overdo it just a little?

Staring at her reflection, Brittany absently dragged the elastic band from her ponytail and shook her head to make her hair cascade to her shoulders. She blinked, then frowned. "Why did I do that?" she asked the woman in the mirror.

But she knew why. She wanted to be sexier for Jake. And her secret pride was her thick, vibrant, shining hair.

A moment later, as she was fishing her hairbrush from her handbag, Brittany saw Karen Blackwell walk into the washroom. Great, Brittany thought. Now she was liable to lose a few fistfuls of her secret pride in a cat fight. How awful. How tacky. Especially since she already felt stupid about the way she'd attacked Karen. Perhaps it would be a good idea to extend an olive branch. "Look, I'm sorry," she said as Karen stood beside her in front of the mirror. "I still think you were all wet to call Jake out on that play, but I was wrong to . . . well, to . . ."

"To come at me like a contender for the pom-pom–weight boxing crown?" Karen said, then astonished Brittany with a grin. "I'm the one who's sorry, Britt. I started baiting you almost from the minute I arrived at the game. And maybe—just maybe, mind you—Jake's toe touched one corner of the plate." She extended her hand. "Cease-fire?"

Brittany readily accepted the handshake. "Of course. But I can't help asking if it was something I did that made you mad at me, and apparently at Jake. Did my goofing around at being a cheerleader bug you? The fact that I obviously knew almost nothing about the game?"

Karen took a compact from her purse and touched up her lipstick and blusher. "My lousy mood had nothing at all to do with the game. My boyfriend and I broke up last week after a year of going together, and I'm hurting. I was mad at my brother for conning me into showing up to umpire the game instead of spending another night crying into my pillow, and when I saw the way you and Jake . . . well, the way you are . . . I gave in to self-pity and took it out on you. It wasn't very mature of me."

"Please, don't give it another thought," Brittany said, then couldn't help adding, "What do you mean, the way Jake and I *are*?"

Karen put away her compact and started toward the washroom door. "In case you haven't noticed," she said in a mock-conspiratorial tone, "you two are nuts about each other. And if you want some advice from the lovelorn, enjoy what you have while you have it. Sometimes it doesn't last, and regrets without the memory of even a little pocket of happiness are such a waste."

Moments later, when Brittany returned to the table, she gave Jake a distracted smile as she sat down beside him. Karen's words had hit home. And maybe they would offer comfort some bleak day when comfort was needed.

"Everything okay?" Jake asked quietly, his glance taking in Brittany's changed hairdo. A sudden flame in his eyes suggested his approval.

Brittany nodded. "Karen and I called a truce."

"That's good. I hate it when women fight over my slo-pitch stats," Jake said with a grin.

Laughing, Brittany stole a peek at Garth. He was talking to someone else, so she remarked to Jake in a low voice, "Everything seems peaceful enough here. Aren't we awfully, awfully civilized?"

"On the surface perhaps," Jake said, reaching up to slide his hand under her hair and rest it on the nape of her neck. "But underneath? That's a different story."

"Is it?" Brittany whispered. His touch seared like a brand. "Under that smooth surface of yours, does the civilized gentleman give way to the primordial male?" she asked, knowing the question was provocative.

"Who knows?" He smiled, a gleam of challenge in his eyes. "Would you care to explore the question a little farther?"

She glanced around at the others. "Not here," she said, realizing she wasn't sure what Jake was capable of doing. All at once her breath was labored, her heart pounding at breakneck speed, her limbs heavy with languid warmth.

He lowered his hand and held it out to her as he got to his feet. "My sentiments exactly, sweetheart."

Brittany took his hand and held on for dear life as she followed him on shaky legs, remembering only when they were halfway to the door of the pub to turn and wave good-bye to the others.

No one seemed surprised by their abrupt exit.

"What's with you and Garth Porter?" Jake asked in the car on the way to Brittany's place.

Even through her sensual haze she heard the edge under his casual question. Because her emotions were as taut as an overtuned violin string, she felt a sudden vibration deep within her and told herself it was indignation, not a thrill of feminine satisfaction. Certainly not that. "I didn't realize we were talking about being uncivilized in *that* particular way," she commented. "Do I hear a note of male territorialism in your question?"

"More than a note, sweetheart," Jake answered pleasantly. He reached across the car seat to trail his fingers over her bare thigh before returning his hand to the steering wheel. "But not because I'm worried about the competition. You don't like Porter. I mean you *really* don't like him, and while I grant you he doesn't seem overly popular with anybody, I'm curious about the extent of your antagonism. Has he done something to offend you? An unwelcome pass, for instance?"

"Oh, sure," Brittany said absently, preoccupied with the effect of Jake's touch. She looked at his hands. They seemed ordinary enough. Better-shaped then some, and larger than most. But normal. Yet their power to arouse her was astonishing. "The occasional clumsy pass wouldn't make me dislike anyone that much, though," she added, remembering to finish her answer. "Garth is a back stabber, with his knife usually poised between Helena's shoulder blades. He happened to inherit shares in several companies when his father died a couple of years ago, including a sizable block in Danforth Developments, so he figures he's qualified to take over from Helena as CEO. He undermines her at every turn. Trying to wear her down, I guess, hoping she'll get fed up enough to throw in the towel and retire. Sometimes I worry that he's succeeding, and I don't want that to happen. Helena took on the leadership of the corporation reluctantly, but she's risen to the challenge, and now she thrives on the work. What's more, she's competent. Garth's not. He's just a big, spoiled kid."

Pulling up at a red light, Jake turned to stare at Brittany. He'd heard everything she'd said, but he mentally filed most of it and zeroed in on her first comment. "'Oh, sure'?" he said, echoing her words and offhand tone. "I ask if some character has made a pass at you, and you say, 'Oh, sure,' as if a clumsy pass is par for the course?"

"Well, I *am* in the hotel business," Brittany pointed out. "Naturally I run into that sort of thing a lot. It's the traveling-salesman syndrome. Men on the road are a strange breed. Put them alone in a hotel room, and their hormones leap into overdrive. They think all the rules are suspended and every passing female is fair game."

"Do they, now," Jake said, his voice laced with irony.

Brittany realized too late that she was talking to the ultimate traveling man. Apparently her brain wasn't working very well. But then, it never did function properly when Jake Mallory was around. "I'm not talking about you. You're single," she mumbled, embarrassed.

"So it's all right if I regard every passing female as fair game, is that it?"

"More likely every passing female regards you as fair game," Brittany shot back.

"Thanks for the compliment, sweetheart. But it seems you're harboring a few prejudices I'm going to have to overcome if I'm to win your wholehearted trust."

Brittany remained silent. She trusted Jake, she told herself. Enough to make love, anyway. Enough to let down all her defenses. Most of her defenses.

"Never mind," Jake said, reaching a hand toward her again, this time to trace the outer rim of her ear with his index finger. "I'll take on your prejudices about me. All of them. And I'll knock them into a cocked hat one by one."

They were quiet for the rest of the short drive and spoke very little in the elevator on the way up to her apartment.

Brittany's nerves were stretched to the breaking point. She was pulsating with anticipation. Just standing next to Jake, feeling the warmth emanating from him, wanting him to touch her . . . She frowned. Why wasn't he touching her? Why wasn't his hand resting on her waist or her shoulder or the small of her back? Why wasn't he tormenting her with his lazy caresses the way he'd been doing all evening? Had he changed his mind about making love to her?

The elevator stopped. Brittany stepped into the hallway and strode briskly toward her door, refusing to let Jake see how unsure she was, how confused, how badly shaken.

But he did see. She couldn't control the trembling of her hand when she tried to fit her key into the lock. "Damn!" she whispered. The same thing had happened to her the last time Jake had stood waiting for her to open her door.

Jake closed his hand over hers and took the key. "How do you manage to get into your apartment when I'm not around?"

"I don't have the problem when you're not around," she admitted, then shook her head in dismay. "You're so calm. So unshakably cool. You . . ." She hesitated but couldn't keep herself from blurting out, "Why did you stop touching me?"

"I had to," Jake answered, his voice suddenly rough with emotion. "I'm *not* calm or cool. All of a sudden, touching you in relatively innocent ways wasn't enough." He pushed the door open and followed her inside.

Another tense silence fell as he put down her club bag, closing the door behind them.

They gazed at each other, countless questions unspoken. But Jake's eyes, coal-dark, caressed Brittany with such erotic promise, she felt as if he were making love to her already. Her lips curved in a shy smile. "Would you . . . would you like a drink before . . ." She stopped abruptly, her cheeks flaming. She was so clumsy, she thought. So transparent. So *impatient*.

Jake chuckled. "No thanks, sweetheart. Not before." Reaching for her and enfolding her in his arms, he added softly, "But maybe after."

Eight

When Jake claimed Brittany's parted lips, she felt a sudden inner release, as if a dam had been breached and her passion were spilling through the opening in a triumphant torrent.

His mouth was hot and demanding as his hands moved over her, molding her to him, setting her on fire. He murmured her name again and again in a husky, loving litany.

As he lifted her in his arms, she clasped her hands at the nape of his neck and nuzzled into the spicy warmth of his throat. She loved that special spot and thought of it as hers alone.

Jake carried Brittany to her bedroom effortlessly, though he felt his heart pounding as violently as if he were under a tremendous strain. Her guileless sensuality was setting off minefields of erotic explosions inside him. She nibbled his earlobe and told him how much she ached for him; she lapped at his skin like a kitten at a saucer of cream. His Kitten. Unaware how easily she could push him over the brink, or how a hunger left unappeased for much too long could edge him past the outer reaches of his self-discipline, she was tempting him with sweet samples of the banquet ahead.

As they entered the bedroom, Jake felt the caress of a cool breeze from the open window, spiced by the ubiquitous scent of cedar that drifted in past the billowing white lace curtains. A pink-shaded lamp in a far corner had been left on, spilling a rosy glow over the white comforter on the brass bed. "You keep a night-light burning when you go out?" he said with a smile, somehow not surprised that Brittany would leave that kind of welcome-home for herself.

"I don't like walking into dark bedrooms alone," she admitted, tipping back her head to smile up at him, her eyes dark and heavy-lidded.

"You're not alone tonight, love," Jake said, setting her down beside the bed and once again clasping her small, slender body to him. "And at long, long last," he added as he stroked her silky hair, "neither am I."

Brittany closed her eyes and slipped into a realm of pure sensuality as Jake's mouth moved over hers, parting her lips with gentle persuasiveness.

Sliding his hands under her shirt, he glided his palms lightly and slowly over her back, his touch at once soothing and stimulating, sending shivers of delight playing over her skin.

Brittany was mesmerized as she helped Jake ease her out of her shirt. She wondered vaguely why a tiny smile tugged at the corners of his mouth when he reached out to follow the scalloped edges of her lacy bra, his fingertips feathering over the slopes of her breasts.

"You're so feminine," he said as he traced every tiny petal and graceful leaf of the lace design until it seemed as if the delicate fabric might not be able to contain the hardening and swelling of her nipples.

Curving his hands over her shoulders, he turned her so that her back was to him, then put his arms around her and cupped her breasts in his palms. He bent his head to rub his cheek against her hair and breathe in its elusive scent of wildflowers.

Brittany could feel the tension vibrating in Jake and knew he was battling to keep a tight rein on himself. Yet she was confident his self-mastery would win out. She remembered his unbelievable control, his almost-mystical knowledge of her body's responses, his uncanny ability to wait, and wait, and wait until she was fulfilled many times over before he sought his own release. He would be patient, and gentle, and loving. He would take care of her in every way. He would make her feel precious and . . . at least for these perfect moments . . . he would make her feel loved.

He unsnapped the hook at the front of her bra and very slowly slid the satin straps down her arms until the wisp of lace dropped to the floor, then filled his palms with her unfettered breasts. He pressed kisses to her shoulders and upper back, then along her spine from top to base, deftly ridding her of her shorts and lace bikini panties in the same smooth movement. Then he straightened up and stepped back a pace. "Don't move," he ordered softly, walking around her in a circle and gazing at her as if she were a work of art. "You're so lovely, Brittany. So beautiful and desirable. And I'm still having such a hard time believing you're real, I just want to look at you."

"And if I want to look at you?" Brittany said, the words low and throaty.

Jake smiled and without a word stripped off his clothes.

Brittany breathed a shuddering sigh. "You're even more glorious than I remembered."

He returned to her and once again drew her back against him within the circle of his arms, letting his hands play lightly over her breasts and stomach.

"Jake," Brittany murmured as she felt his rampant maleness pressing on the base of her spine, hot and rigid and throbbing with life. "Oh, Jake, I want you. I want you so much I can't bear it." She responded with heady joy to his vibrant masculinity, thrilled to the tautness of his thighs, the breadth and velvety hardness of his hair-covered chest, the calluses on his fingers and palms.

"You know how much I want you, Kitten," he whispered with his lips close to her ear. "I've had a thousand dreams of being with you this way again."

"I've dreamed of you too," Brittany admitted, arching her body in an undulating movement as if to follow the leisurely stroking of his hands. "I haven't spent a single night in my bed without wishing you were with me, Jake. I've been such a fool, for such a long, wasteful time."

"Not a fool," Jake protested quietly. "Just frightened." He touched his lips to a quivering pulse spot at the inner slope of her shoulder while splaying his fingers over her belly and inching one hand downward, the other up toward her breasts. "Looking back is even more wasteful than squandering precious moments, so let's not do either. We're here now. We're together. And we're making love to each other. Nothing else matters."

A helpless moan rose in Brittany's throat as Jake's fingers pushed through the dark triangle at the apex of her thighs and found her center. She turned her head so that her lips met his, and he took her mouth as if claiming what had always belonged to him, his insistent caresses tormenting her to burning, moist readiness.

Enflamed beyond endurance, Brittany twisted in Jake's arms, clasped her hands behind his neck, and coaxed him over to the bed.

"I see I'm going to have a lot of trouble with you," Jake said in a feigned growl as they stood by the bed. He reached behind her to pull back the comforter and top sheet, giving in to Brittany's sweet determination.

As she pulled him down onto the bed on top of her, she gazed up at him, her eyes widening in genuine puzzlement. "Trouble?"

He smiled as he parted her thighs. "Yes, my love, but it's the kind of trouble a man enjoys handling."

Brittany still wasn't certain what he meant, but within seconds she didn't care. Jake began to inflict more of his exquisite torture on her, easing himself into her, then drawing back just when she thought he was going to fill her. He dipped his head and closed his mouth over the peak of each of her breasts in turn, suckling hard on the distended nipples, then soothing them with the liquid warmth of his tongue. The pleasure was mind numbing and seemed to go on forever. By the time Jake was sliding his hands under Brittany's hips to lift her to receive him, she was teetering on the edge of an abyss of pure ecstasy, and when he plunged into her, she was rocked by one shattering explosion after another.

"Baby," he whispered as he held her close. "My beautiful love. I'll never let you go again. Never, ever . . . let you . . ." Suddenly his movements stopped for just an instant, then quickened to an almost violent rhythm, building toward a detonation of his own, triggered by her convulsive contractions. "Brittany . . ." he rasped. "This is it, love. This time

I'm making you all mine. This time you're going to belong to me and never forget it. . . ."

As Brittany arched up to meet his final thrust and spun off with him on a whirling starburst, she knew he was right. She did belong to him. She'd belonged to him from the very beginning. She didn't know how she'd imagined otherwise.

But what that irrevocable truth was going to mean to her future, and Jake's, was something she couldn't think about.

Not yet.

Jake could see that the afterglow of the night's lovemaking had faded by the time Brittany had emerged from her morning shower.

He was still in her bed. Lying on his back with his hands clasped behind his head, he watched her and recognized the warning signs. Her smiles were shy and fleeting, she wasn't meeting his gaze, and she kept clutching the lapels of her robe together, making sure it was wrapped tightly around her.

For a moment Jake wished he'd climbed into the shower with her so that she'd have had no opportunity to start second-guessing her feelings, but he realized he couldn't depend forever on lovemaking to keep doubts at bay. The trouble was, he hadn't had much practice at unraveling the tangled secrets of a sensitive woman's emotions.

Okay, he thought. Fine. He didn't know exactly how to deal with Brittany's morning-after fears. But he'd had experience with situations not too different. After years of insinuating himself into all sorts of cultures in order to get a job done, he learned how to blend in, taking part in daily routines until his presence was accepted as natural. He had to follow the same principles with Brittany.

"Do we go for a walk first, then head for the Starting Gate for breakfast, or is it the other way around?" he asked matter-of-factly as he watched Brittany yank her damp hair up into an elastic terry-cloth band.

Brittany froze, staring at Jake in the dressing-table mirror. She'd been bracing herself for this moment ever since the first blast of water in the shower had made her wake up to the many consequences of her night's surrender. The very first consequence was that she would have to figure out how to explain Jake to her friends at the diner. At such an early hour they were bound to know she'd spent the night with him. Not that it mattered of course. She was a grown woman. But . . .

"Brittany?" Jake prompted, wondering if he'd made a mistake. He hadn't meant to throw her into a state of shock.

She managed one of her fleeting smiles. "I usually stop at the diner first, then go for my walk," she answered. "But we could eat breakfast here. I mean, don't feel you have to come al—"

"Your routine sounds great," Jake cut in, getting up to head for the shower. "I'm curious about this famous diner that seems so popular around here. And I'm hungry."

Brittany's forced smile faded as soon as she was alone. She couldn't fathom her reactions this morning. She was glad Jake wanted to join her for breakfast and a walk. She loved being with him. She wanted to enjoy every possible second of his company while he was around. So why was she so edgy?

Perhaps, she conceded reluctantly, it was because

her life had undergone a profound change overnight—but a temporary one.

Jake's life—his real life—would take him else-
where all too soon.

On the way to the diner the conversation between
Jake and Brittany was stilted, punctuated by long
silences.

As she was swinging along beside him in her
yellow track suit, she suddenly said, "You understand, of course, that no one can belong to another
person. Not really."

Jake felt as if someone had just switched on a
light. So the problem was his choice of words. He'd
given Brittany cause to worry about her independence. Knowing how important that sense of
autonomy was to her, he wished he'd been more
careful, but being careful had been impossible at
the time. And now, how could he backtrack? To say
he hadn't meant she belonged to him in a literal
sense wouldn't help. To suggest that he felt he
belonged to her as well would seem phony at this
point.

Finally he decided to brazen it through. He
grinned. "What's wrong with belonging?"

"The very word is what's wrong. It implies owner-
ship. It suggests a . . . a form of enslavement."
Brittany winced even as she spoke, realizing she was
resorting to inflated political rhetoric instead of saying what was actually on her mind.

"You don't think I'm enslaved?" Jake said.

Brittany caught her breath. The man did have a
way of disarming her, she had to admit. Nevertheless
she forced herself to forge ahead, trying to get to the
real point. "I just want to make it clear that things

said in . . . in the throes of passion . . . shouldn't be taken too seriously. You're as free now as you were yesterday, and . . . and so am I."

They'd reached the diner, and Jake held open the door for her. "Whatever you say, Kitten," he murmured as she strode past him into the bright little eatery that was her favorite neighborhood hangout.

Kitten. A flush appeared over Brittany's face and throat. That name again. All Jake had to do was drop it into a conversation and she was inundated by a rush of sensual images that blurred her thinking.

"Interesting place," Jake commented as he looked around the diner at the photographs of legendary racehorses and famous riders. Brittany had told him that a retired jockey named Smiley, along with his wife, Ruby, owned the Starting Gate; they not only offered the best food in town but treated their customers like family.

Family, Jake mused. Brittany had a love of family in any form. No wonder she was rattled by the word *belong.* The feeling was as essential to her as breathing. Like most people, she feared most what she wanted most.

It struck Jake that Brittany would be a wonderful mother. Loving, practical, full of fun . . . The stray thought startled him. It wasn't the kind of thing that normally crossed his mind.

A second thought followed on the heels of the first as Jake realized it was his turn to be rattled: Did he, too, fear the very things he wanted?

Hastily he turned his attention to the Lucy Ricardo look-alike behind the diner's counter who was grinning at Brittany. "Well, now, sweetie," the woman said, subjecting Jake to a fast but thorough once-over without faltering for a second in her flapjack flipping. "Don't you look all bright-eyed and bushy-tailed this morning?"

Jake's grin broadened as Brittany slid onto one of the stools, the color in her cheeks deepening to scarlet. "Hi, Ruby," she murmured, then indicated Jake with a small hand gesture as he sat down beside her. "This is Jake Mallory. He's heard so much about your home cooking, he decided to give it a try."

Neatly done, Jake thought while he and Ruby exchanged pleasantries. He'd been wondering how Brittany would introduce him. Lover? Friend? A guest at the Somerset? He found her self-consciousness refreshing and endearing.

Ruby slid the flapjacks onto a plate and served them to a pin-striped businessman buried behind a newspaper at the end of the counter, sauntered over to Jake, and looked him over more closely. "I'll bet you've got a hearty appetite, Jake Mallory. Not like this little girl, who thinks one oatmeal cookie and a glass of milk is enough to kick-start her for the kind of long, crazy day she usually puts in. I pack a pile of nutrition into those cookies, but there's only so much I can do. What can I get for you, Jake?"

"Ruby, I hate to tell you," Jake said almost sheepishly. "The fact is I normally have fresh fruit and herbal tea, except on days when I go all out and spring for half a grapefruit, a poached egg on dry wheat toast, and black coffee."

"Say it ain't so!" Ruby wailed. "I thought I had me a lumberjack appetite to feed when I saw you walk in, Jake! You sure you won't try one of my deluxe omelets and sausage with whole-wheat biscuits? I cook 'em good and lean. Or lean and good, however you want to look at it."

Lean and good, Brittany repeated to herself. A

perfect description of Jake. Her glance flickered appreciatively over him.

"Okay, Ruby, I'll put myself in your hands," Jake said, wondering about the glint of sensual mischief he'd seen for a brief moment in Brittany's brown eyes.

Ruby began whipping up some concoction, beaming at Jake. "Where'd you find this hunk?" she said to Brittany. "I thought Duke Wayne was the last of the breed. Say, didn't the Duke play the part of a Jake once? Big Jake?"

"He did, in a movie of the same name," Brittany answered, then grinned at Jake. "I think you've just been given your nickname. They do that here."

"Oh, my Smiley will come up with something more original," Ruby protested cheerfully.

"Probably," Brittany agreed with a laugh. She began to relax about having brought Jake to the diner. Once Ruby got onto one of her pet subjects— food, her husband, or one of her movie heroes—she was less likely to make some blunt remark, like . . .

"So, Brittany, is Jake the reason you're glowing this morning after moping around all week?"

Brittany blinked, hoping she'd imagined what she thought she'd just heard.

Jake's low, choked-off chuckle told her otherwise.

"Moping?" Brittany repeated, her voice strained. "Was I moping?"

Ruby hooted. "Were you moping? I was thinking of spiking your cookies with some of my Smiley's Geritol in case you were anemic, that's how much you were moping."

"What a horrible thought," Brittany said, reaching down to punch Jake's leg with the side of her fist as laughter rumbled low in his throat.

Jake coughed and decided to rescue Brittany by

sidetracking Ruby. "Judging by all the oat bran and low-fat features on your menu, Ruby, you're conscientious about the cholesterol count of your customers."

Ruby glowed and launched into an enthusiastic lecture about the benefits of healthy eating, encouraged by knowledgeable questions and comments from Jake.

Ruby had given Brittany her cookie and milk and was putting Jake's well-heaped plate in front of him when she looked up toward the door. "Well, would you look who's here!" she said with genuine excitement. "The proud parents-to-be. And isn't this a wonderful surprise? How are you feeling, girl? Must be better, if you're out at this hour."

So this was Casey, Jake thought as the new arrivals greeted Brittany and immediately started raving about the effectiveness of the herbal tea she'd delivered the previous afternoon. He was pleased she'd followed through so quickly. She hadn't mentioned dropping off his package to Casey, but he was learning that Brittany wasn't one to discuss her kindnesses. He doubted that she gave them much thought.

Even without the talk of miracle-cure teas, Jake was sure he'd have recognized Casey and Alex McLean. Brittany's descriptions had been perfect. Casey was tall and vivaciously pretty, with wild curly hair the color of apricots. Alex was a dark James Bond type, clearly bewitched by his wife.

Both of them, Jake noticed, were darting speculative glances his way. Whether she knew it or not, Brittany had a roster of guardian angles, all vitally interested in her well-being. He wasn't surprised. He only hoped they would give him their stamp of approval—which wasn't like him at all. He'd never been concerned about what anyone thought of him. He couldn't be bothered trying to fit in socially with any group unless he had to make the effort for the sake of his work.

What was Brittany doing to him?

For one thing, he realized, she was introducing him to her friends. He got to his feet and shook hands with Alex, then turned to Casey. But when he reached for her hand, she leaned forward and planted a kiss on his cheek. "I can't thank you enough, Jake. Those teas, along with the other ideas you gave us . . ."

"Ideas?" Brittany interrupted.

"Some hints I've picked up along the way," Jake answered, grinning. "I included them in the envelope with the list of tea ingredients."

"The acupressure neck-and-back massage was fantastic," Casey said enthusiastically. "Alex followed your instructions to the letter, Jake, and even if the results hadn't been miraculous, the massage itself felt so wonderful, I wouldn't have cared. And that bit about pinching and rubbing the skin between my thumb and forefinger stopped a bout of nausea right in its tracks. Where did you learn all those tricks?"

Brittany watched in amazement as Jake, Casey, and Alex began chatting as if they'd known one another all their lives. They were interrupted only by Ruby's insistence that Jake eat his breakfast while it was hot and that the others give proper attention to the goodies she was serving them.

Jake was magic, Brittany decided. He charmed everyone. He could blend in anywhere, with all sorts of people. No wonder her own response to him was so dramatic. Maybe her surrender to him was nothing special as far as he was concerned. Maybe he'd considered it inevitable. Perhaps she was, after all, merely the woman for him in this particular port.

And yet . . . the way he'd said she belonged to him . . . Would he say such a thing if he didn't mean it? If she weren't special to him? *Would* he?

Brittany wished she hadn't made such a big thing of that word. Why had she pretended she didn't believe in people belonging to each other? What was the matter with her anyway? And why was she indulging in all this idiotic soul-searching in the first place? Jake was special, he wanted to be with her when he could, and he made her deliriously happy. What more did she need to know?

Nothing, she told herself firmly. *Absolutely nothing.*

Nine

The days flew by. A week had disappeared, and then another, before Brittany realized that Jake was becoming an integral part of her existence.

True to his word, he took her to the park and taught her to catch a softball instead of diving out of the way when it flew at her. She learned to like batting practice, though she tended to lose her concentration when Jake stood close behind her, his arms encircling her body and his big hands holding hers in the proper position on the bat. Not to mention his breath tickling her skin as he patiently explained what kind of pitch she should wait for.

He taught her several intriguing Japanese words and phrases not found in the average travel dictionary and used such effective techniques to illustrate their meanings that Brittany told him she would love to learn the same words and phrases in other languages. Much to her pleasure, he obliged.

The self-defense moves he insisted she learn finally won her enthusiasm when she found that they invariably ended with a tumble to the floor. She devised all sorts of unorthodox ways to flip Jake onto his back and make him her helpless victim. "You're good," he rasped after one particularly . . . unusual session. "You're so good, you should be awarded a special belt."

"What color? A brown belt?" she murmured as she nibbled his ear. "Maybe even a black one?"

He wrapped his arms around her and rolled so that she was under him. "A pink one," he said, his eyes dark with desire. "Meaning you've mastered the most lethal moves of all."

Brittany smiled and clasped her hands behind his neck, drawing him down so that she could capture his mouth.

"But, sweetheart," he growled, "don't even think about using those tricks on anyone but me."

They went to movies and ate popcorn. They played tennis every second morning at the courts in Stanley Park. They helped Casey and Alex wallpaper a room and paint their back fence, then spent the evening with them eating pizza and playing charades.

When Brittany was working, Jake continued going to the gym and sharing tea and long conversations with Helena. A few hours a day he hefted boxes of canned goods to do his bit for a local food bank. Trudy always had a joke to share with him, and he invariably tried to top it with one of his own. He continued winning games for the Hotshots while Brittany cheered him from the sidelines. He was finding his own niche and settling into it.

It was all so ordinary, Brittany couldn't help thinking from time to time. This kind of life must seem so uneventful to Jake. Yet he seemed to get a kick out of everything they did together and everything he was involved in on his own. Perhaps there was novelty for him in the commonplace. She couldn't help wondering how long it would take for the newness to wear off, but in the meantime she reveled in every blissful moment.

They cuddled together on her oversize couch to watch the videos she rented—favorites she hoped Jake would like as well. He did, and she enjoyed them all the more for having shared them with him.

A wok appeared in her kitchen, along with some strange vegetables and fruits and spices she'd never heard of before. Then herbal teas and flatbreads and goat cheeses. Jake cooked exotic dishes that delighted Brittany. She cooked hamburgers he claimed were the best he'd ever tasted.

"You're gaining weight," she said at the end of their third week together, when they were sharing a shower and she was in a position to notice the slightest change in his body.

"Should I go on a diet?" he asked, picking up the soap to lather her.

She smiled. "Don't you dare. You're perfect. And you're being coy, Jake Mallory. Vain and coy. We both know you've been working on that gorgeous body to get it back to this point. You've also got your beautiful tan back. . . ." She smiled mischievously and trailed her fingers downward over his flat, hard belly. "Well, except for this one area of course."

He drew a sharp breath and lost his hold on the soap.

When it slid to the floor of the tub, Brittany knelt to pick it up. "You have wonderful legs," she murmured, proceeding to lather his calves, then his thighs . . .

Jake's wonderful legs were shaking by the time she straightened up. "And you," he said as he held her against him and let the water stream over them both, "have the sweetest lips in all creation."

Jake started working on the contract he'd taken, spending the better part of most weekdays at a construction site on the east side of the city. But he usually returned to the Somerset in plenty of time to shower and change before Brittany was ready to leave for the day. The routine was comfortable. He started to think normal life—or what most people considered normal—wasn't bad. Not bad at all.

Another contract offer came his way. He could begin as soon as he finished the current one, and the job would need his input for six months. "There seems to be a lot of work for me around this area," he said as he and Brittany were lounging in her living room on a lazy Friday night wearing cutoffs and tank tops, sharing a pot of herbal tea before doing the supper dishes. He told her about the new offer.

Brittany didn't know what to say. The prospect of adjusting to life without Jake was unbearable, yet she couldn't feel right about wanting him to take whatever contracts he could scare up in Vancouver. She knew he had his pick of assignments all over the world. He'd mentioned a few of them before, carefully watching her reaction just as he was doing at the moment, as if testing the waters.

She picked up their empty cups and put them on the serving tray with a clatter of china and silverware. "Wouldn't you prefer to take the project in West Germany? Or the one in New Zealand?" She beetled out to the kitchen with the tray before Jake could answer.

He followed her, eyeing her trim figure. "Have I

mentioned, sweetheart, that you have the best legs in Vancouver?"

She managed a fleeting smile. "Apart from yours, that is."

"Would you go with me if I did accept one of those contracts?" Jake asked.

Brittany began stacking plates in the dishwasher, her moves quick and jerky, "Go with you? Just up and quit my job? Become a . . . a camp follower?" She shook her head. "It wouldn't work. You know it wouldn't. You've said yourself that some of those sites are men-only places."

"Okay, so I'll accept the contract here. No big deal," Jake said, rinsing the wok he'd used to make a shrimp stir-fry.

"It *is* a big deal!" Brittany insisted. "You—"

"Careful, honey, you nearly broke that saucer, jamming it into the rack that way."

Brittany frowned, took a deep breath to calm herself, then carefully placed another saucer in the rack. "The thing is, career sacrifices for the sake of . . . of love affairs . . . invariably turn out badly," she said in the most reasonable tone she could muster. "And what happens after six months?"

"Setting aside my quarrel with your use of the phrase *love affair* to describe what's between us, Brittany, I have to point out to you that I've spent years working my butt off to get to a position where I can pick and choose assignments. We're not talking about my turning down a big chance, or taking a cut in my fee, or settling for a boring project. Now or six months from now, we're talking locations. Nothing more. Geography. Why are you so hung up about it?" Grabbing a damp dishcloth, Jake wiped the countertop with wide, vigorous strokes, adding, "Or *is* it geography that really bothers you?"

"Meaning?" Brittany asked as she straightened up, her hands on her hips.

"Meaning that this business of my travel is a red herring. I thought we'd cleared it out of the way a long time ago, but it doesn't matter. It's not the real issue, and you're not being honest with either of us. You want me to take the contract here, but you won't say so. You won't take that responsibility."

"Well, now, aren't we the cocky one?" she said teasingly, trying to cover up how shaken she was by Jake's gift for cutting right to the heart of a matter. The man had emotional X-ray vision.

Jake threw down the cloth, grasped her by the shoulders, turned her around, and marched her into the living room ahead of him. "Weren't you renting a furnished apartment here at the time you and I met in San Francisco?" he demanded.

Brittany scowled and peered back at him as if he'd jettisoned most of the furniture in the upper rooms of his mind. "Yes, I was. What on earth does that bit of trivia have to do with anything?"

"You bought all the stuff in this apartment *after* we'd had that night together?" he asked, ignoring her question.

"Yes," Brittany said, more puzzled by the minute. "It was also after I moved to this unfurnished apartment, which was after Helena hired me as manager of the Somerset."

"Look at this place," Jake said quietly. "For crying out loud, *look* at it!"

Beginning to follow the direction of his thoughts, Brittany pressed her lips together and tried to shrug nonchalantly. It wasn't easy, with two very large hands clamped down on her shoulders.

Jake whirled her around to face him. "Doesn't some peculiarity strike you about your decor?"

"Nothing at all," Brittany fibbed, hoping Jake wasn't quite as astute as she suspected.

"You don't find anything telling about furniture that's too big for your apartment and makes you look like Lily Tomlin's Edith Ann?"

"Okay, so I like chairs I can curl up in, and a bed I won't fall out of. . . ."

"And a couch that could sleep six? Admit it, honey. Subconsciously or otherwise, you had me in mind when you went shopping."

It was true, Brittany realized as she fell silent, worrying at her lower lip. When she'd gone out to buy the kind of cozy, feminine furniture she'd had back East, she'd found herself picturing Jake looking for a place to put up his feet. The next thing she knew— even though she hadn't expected to see him again— she was watching a staggering crew of delivery men wrestle various pieces of Paul Bunyan Modern up to her apartment.

"Baby, there are layers and layers to you," Jake said quietly, hunkering down enough to beam his penetrating gaze right into her eyes. "The top layer's easy to deal with. On that level everything's simple and straightforward. You want me, you take me, you give yourself to me. You let me into your life. But underneath you're keeping up your guard. You're holding back. You're waiting to see if it's safe to make a real commitment."

She stared up at him. "Is it, Jake?" she asked softly, "Is it safe?"

"Yes," he answered unequivocally.

Then why haven't you said you love me?

Brittany's eyes widened with shock as the treacherous thought popped into her head. "How can you be so certain?" she asked in place of the real question.

Jake smiled and sighed deeply. "How can you have such doubts?"

"Doubts are easy," she answered, battling disappointment. Jake wasn't mentioning love. He was talking about commitment—for six months. "Getting rid of the doubts," she added softly. "That's what's hard."

Jake sensed her slipping away from him, putting up a new line of defenses. His whole being rebelled against the thought. He felt like shaking her, yelling that he loved her and that she damn well belonged to him; he wanted to demand her total love and trust in return.

But sanity prevailed. Once, many years before, when he'd been very young and naive, he'd told a woman he loved her after she'd given him reason to think she felt the same. But she'd backed away from him. Literally, physically backed away, saying that he was too intense and too dominating, that he expected too much from a woman, that everything about him frightened her.

He knew it was true. He *was* intense and dominating. He *did* expect too much from a woman. But, Lord, he didn't want to frighten Brittany. "I don't have to decide about the contract for a couple of weeks," he said lightly, somehow tamping down his runaway emotions. Smiling, he drew her into his arms and began kissing and stroking her with infinite gentleness. When he felt her body ease and saw the familiar glaze of desire in her eyes, he scooped her up and carried her to the bedroom. "In the meantime, sweetheart, let's see what we can do about those stubborn doubts of yours."

Brittany nestled against Jake on her bed while he slept through the birdsong outside the window announcing another sunrise in a frenzy of chirping.

Tentative shafts of sunlight slipped past the half-open window blinds to spill over Jake's naked torso in rivulets of pale gold, highlighting the bronze glow of his skin and the taut muscles under it.

Idly smoothing her hands over the planes and hollows of Jake's body, Brittany marveled at the extravagant masculine beauty of him, the power and gentleness, the toughness and sensitivity. His very features, even in repose, suggested his quiet but unremitting strength.

His lovemaking the night before had been . . . She wasn't sure just *what* it had been, what had happened, what had made Jake snap. He'd begun with the softest of caresses, the sweetest whispered endearments, the most carefully choreographed dance of love. But gradually his iron control had slipped, then shattered in an explosion of raw passion. Suddenly there had been no leash on his need. He'd taken her, not roughly but with no quarter given.

Brittany smiled, remembering that there'd been no quarter asked. How strange that she hadn't been frightened by the startling change in him. She'd known his kisses to be possessive before, even fierce in demand, but all at once his mouth had started plundering hers with delicious savagery. And his hands . . . dear heaven, the things his hands had done, the way they'd made her feel . . .

Her body still burned, her lips still felt swollen. She rubbed her cheek against Jake's shoulder, the tender inside of her leg against his scratchy thigh.

From the beginning she'd sensed a wildness in Jake, kept in check by the sheer strength of his will. But not last night. Last night he'd stripped away his civilized veneer—and hers.

But she'd found out what Jake had meant when

he'd said he wanted her to give herself to him all the way. She wouldn't be allowed to hold anything back, physically or emotionally. Not for long. To love such a man was to surrender completely to him and to that love, going wherever it took her, accepting whatever consequences it involved.

To love Jake would take courage.

Brittany wondered if she was up to the challenge. She hoped so, because there was no turning back for her now. She did love him.

There, she thought with a strange burst of triumph. She'd admitted it, to herself if not to Jake. She loved him.

Pressing her lips to his nipple and flicking her tongue back and forth over it, she stroked him with tentative fingertips.

His arms tightened around her. "Sweetheart," he murmured, "what a beautiful way to wake up."

Brittany smiled. "And how beautifully you wake up," she said, smoothing a palm over his magnificent torso.

"You're lovely, Brittany," he said, reaching up to touch her tousled hair. "Is it my imagination, or is there really a special glow about you this morning?"

With a throaty laugh she curled her fingers through the springy coils of his chest hair. "A glow is entirely possible, Jake Mallory. It goes with the morning-after smile that just won't quit. Something to do with unprecedented fulfillment, I believe."

His body stiffened as Brittany's hand roamed downward to the crease of his thigh. "You say the sweetest things," he rasped.

"But now let's see what sweet things I can do," she whispered.

He smiled, closed his eyes, and settled back to enjoy whatever ideas she came up with.

He had become her gentle Jake again, Brittany thought. That was all right. He didn't have to be barbaric every time. As she kissed, caressed, tasted, and loved him to her heart's content, she decided that he pleased her either way.

Testing her feminine power, she tormented Jake the way he'd tortured her so many times, drawing him to a peak of need, then easing off. Before he had a chance to catch his breath, she began again, luring him ever closer to a summit she sensed he'd never reached before. He seemed helpless, as if his responses were orchestrated by her. Brittany knew he could tip the balance whenever he wished. His willingness to let her take control drove her to new heights of trust and love and sensual excitement.

Finally she straddled him, smiled, then bent to capture his mouth in a long, intimate kiss.

He cupped the flare of her hips in his two hands as she straightened up and slowly, slowly took him into herself. As she rode him, his quiet groans of pleasure thrilled her. But ultimately she lost control. Waves of ecstasy racked her body and left her weak and trembling. "Jake," she cried out, "Jake, I can't . . . I have no strength left. . . ."

Jake's fingers dug into her flesh as his grip tightened. "That's all right, sweetheart," he rasped. "Just let it happen. Let me do it all now, love. I have enough strength for both of us."

Brittany curled her fingers around his wrists, arched her spine, and threw back her head, Jake carried her over the summit. All the way.

A week after Brittany's inner acceptance of her love for Jake, she still hadn't confessed it to him. The reason she gave herself was that he had a decision to make about the six-month contract, and she felt he should make it without the added pressure of hearing those three power-packed words from her.

Besides, he still hadn't said them to her.

They'd reached a loving deadlock.

She was sitting at a picnic bench in Stanley Park, staring out at the ships anchored in the bay and wondering how soon matters would come to a head. It was Saturday, and she'd had to work because of a large wedding at the hotel. Telling her he wanted to speak privately to her right away, Jake had whisked her out of the Somerset at noon, a wicker basket packed with goodies waiting in the car.

Brittany was on edge. What was Jake going to say? Had he made his decision about the contract? Would he stay or go?

He handed her a chicken sandwich he'd just unwrapped, and began filling a plastic cup with lemonade from a thermos. "You were right about Garth Porter," he said at last, his expression grave.

Brittany gaped at him, her sandwich suspended halfway to her mouth. Garth Porter? When she'd been stewing about what was on Jake's mind, she'd never dreamed it was Garth Porter! "How was I right?" she asked when she'd got over her surprise. "What did I say?"

"That Garth was a back stabber," Jake answered. "That having inherited a sizable block of shares in Danforth Developments, he has his eye on Helena's position as head of the company. That he's undermining her at every turn, trying to wear her down so that she'll throw in the towel and retire—presumably to leave the field clear for him."

Brittany realized that Jake was quoting her almost word for word. "Now I remember," she said with a half-smile. "It was the evening of your first game for the Hotshots. After you'd met Garth at the pub, I rattled on about him in the car. Pretty indiscreet of me, come to think of it. But, Jake, I didn't think anything I said about Garth registered on you. All you seemed interested in was whether the men I meet in my job make passes at me."

"The passes were uppermost in my mind at the time," Jake conceded, "but I heard the rest. Everything you say registers with me, Brittany. You're important to me, so anything that worries you concerns me."

Brittany gazed at him, wondering if he had any idea how he melted her heart when he said such things. "What made you decide I was right about Garth?" she asked softly, choosing to stick to the conversation Jake had started. Otherwise she was liable to climb over the picnic table right into his arms.

"Helena has made some disturbing comments lately," Jake said, trying to ignore his body's response to Brittany's sultry expression. She had a way of looking at him that made all his male instincts leap to attention and drove every thought from his mind except erotic ones.

"Comments," Brittany repeated, then arched her brows as Jake's words sank in. "Disturbing comments? Such as?"

He nodded. "She's mentioned more than once that she's beginning to think seriously about stepping down, perhaps even putting her shares on the open market. She's talked about letting the Young Turks take over because she's tired of battling to hold on to a position she didn't want in the first place. I don't think she really means any of it, but she's getting there."

"But that's just awful, Jake! It means Garth's backbiting is working."

"Garth seems to think so," Jake said.

"He does? How do you know?"

"I've been talking to a lot of local developers and other business types, checking out my prospects here."

Brittany's pulse skipped a few beats. Jake wanted to stay. He was actively looking for clients.

"This morning," Jake went on, "somebody asked me if it was true that Helena would be retiring within the year and Garth taking her place."

"Good heavens, what did you say?"

"I asked where he'd heard the story."

"Garth," Brittany said.

"Garth. It seems he's been counting his chickens."

"Well, he's going to lay an egg," Brittany said furiously. Her expression softened in the next instant as it dawned on her why Jake had wanted to talk to her about Garth. "You're worried that the upshot of it all will be that I'll lose my job?" she said with a smile. "I don't think there's much chance that Helena will hand over the reins of Danforth Developments to Garth, and she's still the majority shareholder, so there's not much he can do beyond trying to erode her confidence. But it's sweet of you to warn me." Jake was so caring, she thought as she gazed at him with a rush of affection. He was so protective, not only of her but of anyone she was close to. She loved him for that. She loved him for so many, many reasons, and ached to tell him so. But it wouldn't be fair. He had to be free to move on. She didn't want to turn her love for him into an anchor designed to hold him down.

After letting himself bask in the glowing warmth of

Brittany's eyes for several long moments, Jake cleared his throat and dragged himself back to the subject at hand. "I wasn't trying to warn you about your job, Brittany. I don't believe Helena would let you go even if Garth got his way and she had nothing left to run but the hotel. I just . . . I wanted to . . ." He stopped, frowning. What he'd intended to do was ask Brittany how she felt about a plan he'd been turning over in his mind for some time. But in struggling to find the right words to tell her his idea, he realized that there were no right words. He had to make his decision on his own. There was a big commitment involved, and it wouldn't be fair to put the onus on Brittany to tell him whether or not he should take the plunge. He had to make up his mind whether he was ready for a total overhaul of his life-style, then fish or cut bait without trying to coax a guarantee from Brittany. He only wished he'd been struck by that thunderbolt before he'd started to talk to her. "I just wondered whether you thought I should tell Helena what Garth has been up to," he said at last, hoping Brittany would accept such a feeble explanation.

"Yes, by all means," Brittany said with a quizzical smile. She was surprised that Jake had asked her advice, but she appreciated his caution. "Helena already knows she can't trust Garth, but if she isn't aware of how blatant he's become, she certainly ought to be told. If nothing else, she'll be mad enough to get back some of her fighting spirit— which is all she really needs."

"And maybe an ally," Jake couldn't resist adding.

Brittany smiled and reached across the table to run her fingertips over the back of Jake's hand. "Nobody could ask for a better ally than Jake Mallory," she said, her voice husky.

Jake caught her fingers, entwined them with his own, and carried them to his lips. For the moment he wouldn't say anything more about the drastic step he was considering. He only hoped Brittany would be happy about it when she found out.

It was the following Thursday morning before Jake could arrange to take time from his work at the construction site to meet Helena in the Trellis Room, and by that time he'd done enough nosing around to have quite an earful to give her about her largest minority shareholder.

He chose a table where he could see most of the lobby and spot Brittany if she zipped by. He had no special reason for wanting to catch a glimpse of her—there was a convention in the hotel, and she wouldn't have time for a break. He simply enjoyed watching the way she flashed from one end of the hotel to the other, as if she were making a serious effort to be in two places at once.

He and Helena ordered iced tea and indulged in small talk until she suggested it was time for him to get to the point.

Jake laughed. He liked her style. "All right, let's talk about Garth Porter."

"What about him?" she asked, her expression revealing nothing.

Oh, yes, Jake thought, *he did like this woman's style.* She had brains and class to spare. It wasn't until he'd filled her in on the rumors Garth had started about her retirement that blue flames flared in her eyes, and when Jake told her he'd learned that Garth had a backer waiting in the wings to help him buy out her shares, she just shook her head. "Thank you, Jake. There's no way I can oust that young man from the Danforth board, but I can make certain he never gets into a majority shareholder position, even after I do retire."

"I was hoping you'd feel that way," Jake said. A slow grin lifted the corners of his mouth, and he leaned forward. "So Helena . . . can we talk?"

They talked. It was an intense conversation that both of them knew was a turning point in Jake's life, and probably in Brittany's as well.

"Then it's a deal," Jake said at last.

"A wrap, as they say," Helena agreed. "Shall we order some more iced tea to drink to the success of our future association?"

Grinning, Jake was about to suggest something a little stronger, when the corner of his eye caught a streak of hot pink whizzing into the lobby from the stairway, homing in on the front desk. His heart leapt into a triple-axle spin. The streak was Brittany in her bright linen dress. Sweet, achingly sexy Brittany, her glorious chestnut hair bouncing on her shoulders with every purposeful stride.

"Oh, Jake," Helena murmured, "you should see your eyes right now. Have you told her how much you love her?"

He hesitated before saying, "Not yet." He couldn't tear his gaze from Brittany. He ached with love for her. He longed to tell her—but was she ready to hear the words? "I haven't even told her about the proposal I just put to you. I didn't want to scare her off or put pressure on her," he said quietly.

Helena shook her head and sighed. "So the young are as foolish and as hamstrung by pride as ever?

Still finding excuses not to risk being the first to put it all on the line?"

Jake's attention veered sharply back to her. "Is that what I'm doing?"

Helena merely smiled.

Ten

As Jake and Helena left the Trellis Room, he kept thinking about what she'd said.

Was he making excuses? Was Jake Mallory, who liked to believe he was as gutsy as any man, *afraid* to come right out and tell Brittany how much he loved her? To say he was not only ready to settle in Vancouver to be with her but had taken the first real step toward making that commitment?

He was almost glad of the distraction when Garth Porter strode through the main entrance into the lobby, sauntered up to Brittany, and dropped a hand onto her shoulder as he spoke to her. The gesture seemed to be a bad habit of Garth's, Jake thought with a surge of irritation. He narrowed his eyes, curled his own hands into fists at his sides, and started forward.

"Don't do it, Jake," Helena said calmly. "Brittany can handle the situation. You may be her white knight as well as mine, but you'll have to learn when to suit up in your armor and when to let your lady-love put the black knight in his place all by herself."

Jake knew Helena was right. He unclenched his fists and took a few deep breaths, watching as Brittany looked down at Garth's hand and spoke quietly. Jake was certain she was saying, "Move it, Garth, or lose it." Garth moved it.

"All right now?" Helena said. "Back in control?"

Jake chuckled sheepishly. "Back in control. Sorry."

"Oh, don't be. I find all that rampant male aggressiveness charming, Jake. It reminds me so much of David. But let's handle Garth the way you've planned, not with the thumping he deserves."

Across the room Brittany glared at Porter and made an abrupt slicing motion in the air with one hand as she spoke sharply to him, then turned away to deal with a convention delegate making a bid for her attention. What she didn't see was Chef Sandro emerging from the kitchen with a mango in his hand and fire in his eyes.

Helena shook her head and laughed. "There are times, Jake, when heading a giant corporation seems infinitely easier than running a small hotel. I don't know about you, my friend, but I'm outta here."

Jake's laugh was more genuine than before as Helena breezed away. Her exit told him just how much faith she had in Brittany.

Jake also had faith in Brittany, but he wasn't going anywhere except to the front desk, where he could be on hand if she *did* need a passing paladin.

Trudy saw him first. "Hiya, Jake," she said with a devilish twinkle in her eyes and a sidelong glance at Garth. "Did you hear the one about the—"

"Jake!" Brittany said, whirling to greet him, her smile brighter than the sun itself.

He loved the way she did that. Whenever he surprised her, even if they'd been together only an hour before, she lit up as if she'd missed him and was thrilled to see him again . . . as if he was the best thing that could happen to her.

He knew she was the best thing that could happen to him.

"Hi there, big guy," Garth said, sounding a little worried.

"Hello, Porter," Jake said without looking at him.

The convention delegate, his question apparently answered, mumbled his thanks to Brittany and wandered off. She was still gazing at Jake. Jake was still gazing at her.

Sandro scooted over to Jake and waved the over-ripe mango under his nose, managing to divert his attention from Brittany. "You think Leonardo used cheap paint? You think Michelangelo wasted his genius on fake marble? You think Sandro cooks with such . . . such garbage?"

Bewildered, Jake looked to Brittany for guidance.

She took control of the situation. "You're so right, Sandro," she said, scowling at the offending mango. "There must have been a delivery mixup. You would never choose fruit that's past its prime. I'll take care of the matter right away. Meanwhile we do have a banquet to prepare, so do you think you could work your special magic with whatever you have that's usable?"

"Sì, bella, for you. Only for you." He turned and beamed up at Jake. "You know you are a lucky man, my friend? Such a woman, this. You take good care of her, capisce? Or you answer to Sandro." Puffing out his chest, he pivoted on one heel and marched back to his kitchen.

Jake wondered if Brittany had any idea how many protectors she had. "You know, I believe that little guy could be dangerous," he remarked with feigned alarm. "I'd better consider myself on notice."

"You'd better," Brittany said, her voice low and throaty.

They stood smiling at each other for several moments more, until a cough from the sidelines reminded them that Garth hadn't gone away. Brittany turned to him. "Was there something else you wanted, Garth?"

He was staring at her in apparent disbelief. "Aren't you interested enough even to hear me out?"

"No, Garth, I'm not."

Garth switched his shocked gaze to Jake. "Maybe you'll listen, pal. See, I've got a line on something for Britt that I think you'd both be pretty pleased with, but she's got a closed mind. I've been doing some pretty good networking for her, and she doesn't appreciate it at all."

"I don't want you networking for me," Brittany put in before Jake could say anything. "I'm happy where I am."

Garth ignored her. "Jake, I'm trying to tell the lady about a plum job that could be hers if she'd go for it. We're talking major league, pal. A buddy of mine owns this big luxury spa, and he wants to put a woman in to run the place. I mean, it's a fantastic career move. Opportunities like this just don't come along everyday, you know."

"Let me repeat it one more time," Brittany said. "I'm happy where I am."

"Wait a minute, Britt. I'm just coming to the best part." Garth grinned at Jake. "Okay, maybe I'm about to get a little too personal here, but let's face it—everybody knows you two are an item. What would you say if I told you the spa happens to be in Santa Barbara?"

Jake hadn't had much chance to say anything so far, but suddenly there was complete silence from Brittany. He glanced over at her and saw that she'd been knocked for a loop. Her eyes were huge and dark as she looked back at him. Suddenly she was faced with a dilemma—or thought she was. He wanted to tell her there was no problem, but he didn't want to spill the beans in front of Garth.

Jake turned back to Garth and resisted the impulse to wipe the smirk off the man's face. "I don't recall telling you I was from Santa Barbara," he said, keeping his expression bland. The remark was irrelevant. He just wanted to give Brittany time to regroup.

It was Garth's turn to be caught off guard. He blustered a bit, then muttered something about having picked up the information somewhere, probably from the hotel staff's gossiping.

In the background Trudy harrumphed indignantly.

Finally Brittany lifted her chin and said, "Garth, don't you feel the least bit guilty for suggesting I quit on Helena?"

"Guilty?" Garth replied. "Why? I have nothing to do with the Somerset. I'm just trying to do a couple of favors—one for a friend who's having trouble finding a good manager and one for a lady who ought to appreciate a big break. What's the problem?"

"Oh, Lord," Brittany said with a deep sigh. "It's like trying to explain music to the tone-deaf. Never mind, Garth. Thank you for the vote of confidence, but I'll pass."

"You're making a mistake, you know."

"Perhaps," Brittany said, afraid that Garth might be right. Would Jake resent her for turning down the chance to move to his town? She wasn't sure. All she could do was hope he would understand why she couldn't leave Helena at this particular time. She took a deep breath, darted a regretful glance at Jake, then said to Garth, "Nevertheless the answer is no. Once and for all . . . no."

"I don't get it," Garth muttered. "I just don't understand."

Jake suppressed a smile of mingled amusement and satisfaction—amusement because he could see that Garth really didn't understand Brittany's unwavering loyalty, and satisfaction because Garth's attempt to undermine Helena by wooing away someone she depended on had failed miserably. Brittany didn't know it, but she'd just set Garth up perfectly for what Jake wanted to do. "What part of the word *no* don't you understand, Garth?" he couldn't resist asking.

Garth opened his mouth, closed it again, then turned on his heel and stalked away.

Jake decided not to make his own move until Garth had spent a couple of days fuming about the impossibility of dealing with people who let integrity get in the way of ambition. "Sorry," Jake said to Brittany, keeping his voice down so that their conversation would be private. "I didn't mean to butt in, sweetheart. I'm sure you'd have preferred to handle Garth on your own, and you were doing just fine. . . ."

"You didn't hesitate," Brittany said, her eyes shining. "You backed me up. Just like that, no questions asked." Suddenly a disturbing thought hit her, and her expression clouded. "Don't you want me in Santa Barbara?"

Jake knew what his answer should be. This was the time when he should tell her about his pact with Helena. But he wanted to present her with a *fait accompli*, so he let his gaze travel over her from head to toe and gave her a lazy smile. "Kitten, I want you anywhere I can get you," he murmured.

Brittany's color heightened as she glanced around her to see whether anyone had overheard. "I'm afraid I'll be working late this evening," she said hastily. "I have no idea when I can get away."

"That's okay. I'll stick around my suite and use the time to catch up on some paperwork. You can call when you're through."

"I'll have to come in for a while tomorrow as well," she added, getting the bad news over with all at once. "So there goes our lazy Saturday."

"We'll find another day to be lazy," Jake said easily. "It's no big deal, okay?"

"No big deal," she said with a sudden grin. "You know, I'm beginning to like that expression." Impulsively she rested her hand on Jake's arm and rose on her tiptoes to kiss his cheek. "I'll call you the minute I'm ready to go home."

Jake's pulse quickened as he felt the softness of her lips and breathed in her familiar floral scent. Only Brittany could inject so much erotic promise into such an ordinary phrase and such a chaste little kiss. "I'll be waiting," he said as he captured her gaze. "Whenever you're ready for me, sweetheart, just let me know."

Brittany smiled and reluctantly returned her attention to her duties, wondering—as she so often did—why she always seemed to hear deeper meanings in the things Jake said to her.

Perhaps, she thought, it was because she wanted to hear those deeper meanings. And she wanted to believe in them.

"You're spoiling me," Brittany said as she stepped out of the bubble bath Jake had drawn for her and let him wrap her in a huge, thick towel.

"Would you prefer not to be spoiled?" Jake asked lightly.

She tipped back her head and gave him a sultry smile. "Do I *look* like a fool?"

"You look like a woman who was born to be pampered but somehow went astray and acquired an overdeveloped work ethic," Jake said with a grin as he swept her up in his arms and carried her to the bedroom, where the rosy glow of the ever-burning night-light welcomed them.

"You know, you could be right," Brittany murmured, resting her head against his broad shoulder and thrusting her fingers through his mat of chest hair. He was wearing only cutoffs, as he usually did when they were alone together at her place, and she never wearied of experiencing his extravagant masculinity in all its textures and warmth and strength.

After setting her on her feet beside the bed, Jake took an inordinate amount of time patting and rubbing her until she was dry.

Brittany didn't offer the slightest protest. Jake had decreed that she was tired after her long day and that the rest of the evening was off-limits to shoptalk. In fact, he'd said, the less talk of any kind, the better. There were other ways of communicating.

"Okay, sweetheart, stretch out facedown on the bed," Jake ordered, tossing aside the towel and pulling back the comforter. "It's back-rub time."

"Decadent," Brittany said. "Absolutely sinful." But she did as she was told, and within moments she had entered a time warp of pure sensual bliss. The crisp sheets were cool against her skin; a gentle breeze whispered through the open window and over the small of her back; and the quiet melodies of Mozart on the bedside radio gentled her spirit.

Jake began smoothing warmed, lightly perfumed

oil onto her neck, shoulders, and back, patiently
working out knots of tension she was sure had been
in place for years. Soon she was sighing with pleasure, not an inch of her body neglected by Jake's
painstaking massage—not her toes, not the arches
of her feet, not the tendons of her heels. Not her
calves or thighs or the flare of her buttocks. Not
her fingers, palms, wrists, or even the insides of her
elbows.

Brittany was limp and malleable by the time Jake
eased her onto her back and began his attentions all
over again, starting at her toes. His touch was firm
but never painful. He drummed his fingertips over
her thighs and belly, then soothed away her flutters
of excitement with a slow gliding of his palms. He
shaped her breasts and rolled their tips between his
thumb and fingers, drawing on them until they were
hot and swollen and aching for the caresses of his
mouth. A new kind of tension, a delicious explosive-
ness, took the place of what Jake had driven out as
he moved his hands downward until his fingers were
splayed over her thighs, then made long sweeping
strokes that inched ever closer to her pulsating
center.

With her breathing growing rapid and shallow,
Brittany made ragged little sounds that were lost in
the recesses of Jake's mouth as it moved over hers.
Then he began the most exquisite torture ever,
covering her with kisses, using his lips and tongue to
transport her to a kind of altered reality.

Hours passed—or minutes. Brittany had no idea
which. At some point Jake shed his cutoffs and
briefs, but she didn't know when or how. She only
knew he was naked, and then he was sliding his
hands under her body to cradle her against him, and
she was arching to welcome his entry. When he filled

her, she heard her own rapturous cries, punctuated
by raspy endearments from Jake.

They whirled in eddies of pleasure toward a vortex
of transcendental joy, tasting the salt of their mingled tears as they reached the world that was all
their own, where no one else could follow.

Afterward Brittany slept in Jake's arms. Holding
her, he knew it was time he took all the risks there
were to take. He had to tell Brittany about his
decision to buy Garth Porter's shares in Danforth
Developments. He had to tell her he'd decided to
turn down the six-month contract because he
wanted something more, because he wanted to start
seeing projects through from concept to completion.
He wanted to build something he cared about.

Most of all he wanted to build a life with Brittany.

First, though, he had to take the biggest risk of all.
He had to tell her he loved her.

He drifted off to sleep trying to decide whether to
spill out everything first thing in the morning or wait
until evening, when he could set the scene for a
proper, old-fashioned proposal.

Then morning came—and with it the phone call
that swept aside all his plans and all his good
intentions.

Brittany stared at Jake, clutching her robe around
her as if it could hold her together and keep her from
shattering into little pieces. "How *could* they? My
God, Jake, how could anyone ask such a thing? It's
insane!"

"It's not as bad as it sounds, sweetheart. Trust me
on this. It's . . ."

"Jake Mallory, if you say it's no big deal, I jus

might throttle you," Brittany cut in, grabbing the ends of her tie belt and jerking the knot tighter.

He gave her a feeble smile. "I thought you were beginning to like that expression."

"Yesterday I was. Today I'm not." Brittany covered her face with her hands and pressed her fingers against her eyelids, pushing back stinging tears. It was irrational to think life was playing a cruel trick, but she couldn't help it. She'd accepted the totality of her love for Jake, and now he was going to leave her, just as she'd feared all along.

Abruptly lowering her hands, she took a deep breath and let it out slowly, then managed to say with forced calm, "Let's have some breakfast. I could use a cup of very strong coffee right about now."

"So could I," Jake said, sighing heavily as he followed Brittany to the kitchen, wondering for a fleeting moment of raw frustration if the two of them simply weren't meant to be together. Now he even had to put off the little chat he'd planned with Garth Porter.

Refusing to give in to defeatism, he told himself that this crisis was just another challenge he had to meet.

With reckless abandon Brittany prepared the coffee maker, then set out plates, cutlery, and small pots of jam in the breakfast nook. Jake got down mugs from the cupboard and put slices of bread in the toaster. Neither of them said a word.

When the toast popped, Brittany snatched it up and threw it onto a plate, swearing and shaking her burned fingers, then grabbed a knife and started trying to slap hard butter onto one of the slices.

So far, Jake thought as he stood beside Brittany feeling helpless, he wasn't doing very well with this

challenge. He couldn't think of a thing to say to ease
the tension.

Suddenly Brittany dropped the knife onto the
counter with a clatter, turned to Jake, and hurled
herself against him, wrapping her arms around his
waist and burying her face in his shoulder. "Tell me
I've misunderstood," she pleaded. "Better yet, tell me
I'm having a nightmare, that the alarm clock will go
off any minute and I'll open my eyes and laugh about
the craziness of bad dreams."

"Listen to me, sweetheart. It *isn't* the terrible
prospect you're imagining."

She pushed herself away from him and went back
to mangling the toast with chunks of butter. "You're
going to fly off to some secret place in the Middle
East and walk right back into the mess you escaped
from, and I'm supposed to believe it's not terrible?"
She picked up the plate of toast fragments and set it
down so hard on the table, Jake was surprised
nothing broke. "Could you explain to me again why
you have to go? How do you know it isn't a trap?
Those damned terrorists will get their hands on you
again, and this time they'll make sure you don't get
away!"

"It won't be like that, sweetheart. In the first place
those so-called terrorists aren't the hardened killers
you hear about in the news. They're teenagers who
grew up in refugee camps, don't see any hope for the
future, and unfortunately got their hands on some
guns they figured would be the answer to all their
problems. When they were holding me prisoner, I got
to know a couple of them pretty well, and I swear
they're not dangerous in a cold-blooded way."

"A hot-blooded way can get you just as dead,"
Brittany said, hardly believing that the man she
loved was leaning against her kitchen counter

calmly talking about . . . about what Jake was talking about! "I think it's reasonable to assume that teenagers in the Middle East who grab an American off the street and hold him hostage aren't trying to force him to play shortstop for their slo-pitch team."

"You're right, but they're bunglers. They have no idea what to do with a hostage if they get stonewalled by the people they're trying to get concessions from—whether it's money, more guns, the release of one of their pals from custody, or media attention. That's why I was able to escape. Hell, those kids probably made it easy. It was either that or kill me or maybe feed me for life, because I'd made a prior agreement with the company I worked for that it wasn't going to give in to any blackmail demands on my account."

"You *what*?" Brittany yelped, grabbing the counter for support as her legs threatened to collapse under her.

"I told them not to give in to blackmail," Jake repeated. "But they were to do everything short of that to free me. So they did. And the guy who risked his own neck to help me make my break is Jerry Morris—the very person who's in trouble now. I can't turn my back on him. Besides, I'm not walking into a trap. I won't be in any danger. I've been asked to act as an adviser to the people negotiating for Jerry's release, and if necessary to the professionals who'll go in after him if the talks break down. They figure I can help because I've been in the same situation Jerry's in, and I'm familiar with the terrain. Also, I know Jerry well enough to have a handle on how he'll react to any given move. I'll be sitting in some cushy office, a hell of a lot safer than I am out on a slo-pitch field with a bunch of crazy Hotshots." He paused, then said quietly, "You do understand why I have to go, don't you?"

Noticing that the coffee was ready, Brittany put off answering by filling the mugs, her hands shaking so much it was all she could do to keep her aim reasonably true. "What I don't understand," she said as she handed Jake his cup, "is why this Jerry Morris person didn't get out of that place when you did."

"He's a journalist," Jake answered, sitting down at the table. "Need I say more?"

Brittany scowled and plunked herself down in the chair opposite him. "No, you needn't say more. I can imagine both Casey and Alex getting themselves into the same kind of mess."

"And you'd be the first one racing to the rescue," Jake pointed out.

"I would not," Brittany retorted.

Jake reached across the table and crooked his finger under her chin to make her face him. "Look me straight in the eye and say that, sweetheart."

"Okay, okay, so I'm as crazy as you are," Brittany conceded. She thought hard for a while, then suddenly brightened. "That's it!"

Jake withdrew his hand, not sure he liked the sound of those two words. "What's what?"

"I'll go with you, Jake. If it's as safe as you claim, it'll be an interesting experience for me, and a whole lot better than sitting around here going out of my mind with worry."

"Cute," Jake drawled. "But if you're serious, honeybunch, forget it."

Brittany cocked one brow at him. "So it's not all that safe? You've been giving me a snow job?"

"For me it's safe enough, but for you . . ." He shook his head and laughed. "Why am I *discussing* such a thing? It's out of the question, and I hope you're joking even to suggest coming with me."

"I hoped you were joking when you told me *you* had to go, but it seems you weren't. I . . ."

"Brittany, stop," Jake ordered gently.

She closed her mouth and glowered at him, realizing he was right. Obviously she couldn't go with him.

"Besides, honey, you're needed here," he said when he saw that she'd accepted the inevitable.

"So are you. What about your contract? The current one, I mean. Can you just walk off the job?"

"No problem. I've wrapped up most of my part of the work, and I can leave instructions for any details I'd have been checking on."

"You're really going to do this," Brittany whispered, her eyes filling with tears.

"I'll come back," Jake said. "I swear it, Brittany." He stopped himself just short of blurting out the words of love he'd planned to say. The timing couldn't be worse. "And right now I have a little while before I have to get ready to head for the airport. How does your schedule look?"

Brittany thought about it for perhaps ten seconds. Then, deciding she didn't want to think anymore, she said fiercely, "My schedule be damned" and all but dragged him back to the bedroom.

Brittany managed not to cry when Jake stopped by her office at the hotel later that morning, packed and ready to hop into a cab. He'd refused to let her drive him to the airport, forgetting himself enough to tell her that they shouldn't let themselves make a "big deal" of this trip of his.

To Jake's relief she'd laughed at his slip of the

tongue. It had been a ragged little laugh, but he'd appreciated her effort.

"I'll try to stay in touch, but I'm not sure whether it'll be possible to call," he said as he held her in his arms, breathing in her fragrance as if it were an elixir to sustain him through the difficult days to follow. "And this whole . . ."

"Mission?" Brittany supplied helpfully, her voice muffled as she pressed her face into the hollow of his throat.

"Okay, we'll call it a mission if it pleases your sense of drama," Jake said, smiling and reaching up to stroke her hair. "In any case it shouldn't take more than a week or two. I'll be back before you know it." Silently offering a little prayer that he was right, Jake tightened his arms around Brittany, bent his head, and captured her sweet mouth in a long, deep kiss.

When finally he had to release her, he strode to her office door and didn't turn back until he'd opened it, ready for a quick getaway. "I'd tell you to keep a light burning in the window," he said, wishing his voice weren't so hoarse, "but you already do. A pink one."

Brittany blinked back the tears that were threatening to spill over. "Then I'll . . ." She hesitated, then managed to say before her throat closed completely, "I'll keep one burning in . . . my heart."

Jake's eyes glazed over as her words nearly got the best of him. Then, without another word, he turned and left while he was still capable of going.

Eleven

Brittany sat with Casey and Alex at the Starting Gate while Smiley, behind the counter, raced to keep up with the orders of a capacity crowd.

Yet the place seemed empty.

Jake had left a void everywhere in Brittany's life since he'd gone away—a void not just at the diner and the Somerset, or on the paths of Stanley Park and the seawall, and not just in her apartment and her bed.

Her insides clenched with loneliness whenever she passed the herbal-tea display in the grocery store, or heard the thwack of tennis balls, or watched youngsters in a sandlot pickup game.

Realizing she was allowing herself to spiral down into a serious case of self-pity, Brittany mustered a cheerful smile. "Casey, you won't believe this, but I played for the Hotshots last night," she said proudly. "Shortstop, no less."

"Why wouldn't she believe it?" Alex asked, leaning on the counter to peer past Casey at Brittany.

"Because I grew up with this little athletic nonsupporter, remember?" Casey answered as she inspected the available selection of muffins. "I spent all my formative years distracting gym teachers whenever it looked as if they were going to discover her hiding behind the backstop. What got into you last night, Britt?"

"Somebody had to take Jake's place," Brittany explained, then added softly, "and I wanted to be able to tell him I'd done it."

Blinking back sudden tears, Casey gave Brittany's shoulder an affectionate mock punch. "Good stuff, kiddo. How'd it go?"

"I caught a pop fly, and I had one base hit. The Hotshots won. Everybody made a special effort so that we could tell Jake we'd done him proud." Brittany laughed huskily. "He certainly leaves his mark, doesn't he? By now he probably has all the political tensions in the entire Middle East smoothed out. After all he's had nearly two weeks."

"Have you heard from him since his call the night before last?" Alex asked.

Brittany shook her head, distractedly breaking her cookie into tiny pieces and dropping them on her plate. "He told me not to expect any more contact for at least another week. It seems those international Dead End Kids are playing convoluted cat-and-mouse games, one day agreeing to meet with the negotiators and the next saying they don't trust them. He says the powers-that-be are going crazy. They'd rather deal with seasoned terrorists than hotheaded amateurs. Too unpredictable for comfort, I guess." She was silent for a long, pensive moment, then said very quietly, "What scares me is that if Jerry Morris isn't released soon, Jake will do whatever it takes to go in and get him. He hasn't said as much, but I know Jake. He won't leave his friend to sweat it out indefinitely."

"And if I know Jake," Alex said, "he won't do anything stupid even if the powers-that-be you're talking about would allow it. He wants to come back to you, Britt, and he will."

Brittany smiled as if she believed it, but deep down she wasn't sure. Not only was she terrified something would happen to Jake, she couldn't help wondering if this daring adventure would turn out to be like a shot of bourbon to an alcoholic. It was possible he'd found out already that he couldn't live without the excitement and constant change of scenery he'd been used to all his life, and she couldn't bear to be the person who fenced him in. For all she knew, he was wondering at this very moment how to tell her he'd realized he couldn't settle down after all—and couldn't take her with him where he was going.

"What you need is a change of scenery," Casey said, breaking into Brittany's thoughts. "Alex and I are taking the ferry over to Vancouver Island later today to spend the weekend combing the antique shops in Victoria for a cradle. Since you won't be hearing from Jake anyway, why don't you come along?"

Brittany laughed. "It's sweet of you to ask, but Helena got to me first. She wants an inventory done on the contents of her country house up the coast, and ages ago I gave her a standing offer to do the job. She and David bought the place just before he died, so they never lived there. Still, it's only now that she has the heart to sell it, and all of sudden she wants the inventory right away. Her impatience couldn't have anything to do with giving me something to occupy my mind of course."

Casey chewed thoughtfully on a bit of banana-strawberry muffin, then slanted Brittany a troubled look. "Are you sure you want to be by yourself in such an isolated spot, Britt? Is there a telephone?"

"I'm sure, Case. And no, there's no phone in the house, but I can make calls or collect messages at a store down the road." Brittany glanced at her crumbled cookie and then at her watch. "Now that I've finished my milk and disintegrated my breakfast, I'm off. Good luck with the cradle shopping."

After getting up and striding toward the door, she glanced back and rolled her eyes as she saw Casey's worried expression. "Stop looking that way, Case! I'll be fine!"

"And so will Jake," Alex said firmly.

Brittany faltered for just an instant, then grinned and hurried away.

Calling up a shot of adrenaline from his depleted reserve, Jake burst through the side door of the Somerset's lobby and zeroed in on the front desk as if it were a strategic target. "Is Brittany around here, Ron?" he asked after a brief nod of greeting to the weekend clerk.

"Hi, Mr. Mallory. I didn't know you were back," the eager college student said, leaping to his feet. "Did you have a successful business trip?"

"Very," Jake answered, glad to find that the real reason for his absence wasn't general knowledge. "I tried to call Brittany from the airport, but there was no answer at her place. I thought she might be working."

"Not here. She's at Mrs. Danforth's country house, about an hour up the coast."

Jake was disappointed. As soon as he'd got the news that Jerry had been freed in a surprise capitulation, he'd thought about nothing but getting back to Brittany. He'd flown halfway around the world in record time by taking whatever weird connections he could get, and she was still another hour away. He thought about the comfortable bed in his suite. He was exhausted. Every bone in his body ached, but his spirit ached even more. He would dredge up a little more energy rather than wait to have Brittany in his arms. "Ron, do you have a phone number for Helena's house?" he asked.

"'Fraid not," the clerk answered. "There isn't a phone. Britt's been calling in for her messages, and I just heard from her about half an hour ago. But Mrs. Danforth's upstairs. Maybe she'd know some way to get in touch if it's important."

"It's important," Jake said. He picked up the house phone and punched out the number of Helena's suite, willing her to answer quickly.

She did, and minutes later Jake was racing out to the parking lot for his car, the directions to the country house in his pocket.

He started on the last leg of his personal quest feeling only his own pressing need to see Brittany, to hold her again, to know she was real and his. He wanted to tell her all the things he'd been storing up for days or weeks . . . or perhaps a lifetime.

It wasn't until he was within minutes of his destination that an inexplicable, ominous chill swept over him.

Brittany needed him. Jake had no idea how he knew. He just did. He had to get to her. Something had happened, or was going to happen unless he could prevent it.

He prayed he would reach her in time.

Brittany was sitting in one of two wicker peacock chairs on the wide veranda of Helena's sprawling stone house, taking a lemonade break from the painstaking list she was making of the possessions handed down from times long past.

She'd expected a haphazard storehouse of forgotten antiques, but she'd found treasures under the protective sheets, all in place for a gracious existence that had been cut short when fate had stepped in with a tragic change in plans. A lump rose in Brittany's throat every time she thought about Helena's courageous adjustment to life without David.

From her vantage point on a high bluff backed by a dense forest and overlooking the ocean beyond the highway below, Brittany tried to concentrate on the reassuring timelessness of the mountain-studded sea, the pungent scent of evergreen after a late-morning downpour, the heat of the summer sun soaking into her tense muscles.

"Stay safe, Jake," she whispered into the breeze. "Whatever you do, whatever you want when all this is over, please just stay safe."

Taking a deep breath to get control of herself as her eyes filled with tears, Brittany picked up a photo album she'd found in a box of keepsakes and began leafing through it. She easily picked out snapshots of a very young Helena and David.

She was halfway through the album when tears started spilling uncontrollably down her cheeks. Snapping the photo album shut and setting it aside, she jumped up and muttered, "Stop wallowing in misery, Brittany Thomas. Jake deserves better from you." Deciding to go for a walk, she bounded down the veranda steps, around the side of the house, and onto a path toward the woods.

Within moments she was ducking under a low-hanging tree branch and picking her way along the narrow, rain-muddied, rock-strewn trail, swiping angrily at her tears with the back of her hand. She charged through the thick undergrowth, eager to reach an idyllic spot she'd discovered the day before: a flat rock jutting out over a fast-running river that sliced through the hillside in a rush of white water and high-leaping trout.

She'd been walking for about five minutes when she reached the part of the path that sloped sharply down to the riverbank. Suddenly the toe of her sneaker caught in an exposed root, and a shaft of pain shot up from her ankle. As her knees buckled, she pitched to one side and began rolling down the slippery embankment toward the torrent below.

"Jake!" she cried out automatically, then gasped as her head glanced off a boulder near the river's edge. "Jake, help me!"

Plunging into the frigid water, Brittany accepted the awful truth that Jake, for the very first time since he'd come back into her life, wouldn't be there when she needed him.

But she kept hollering for him anyway.

She was hallucinating, Brittany told herself. She'd knocked herself silly on that boulder. She'd been hanging onto the fragile overhanging branch too long, battered by the icy current. No other explanation was possible. She'd wished so desperately for Jake to appear out of nowhere to rescue her, she'd managed to conjure up a vision of him. A running, shouting, clambering-down-the-hillside hologram of Jake.

Her body—most of it in the water—was half-frozen, her mind numb with shock. Refusing to give in and be dragged over jagged rocks and dead trees to where the water was deep enough for her to drown, she had a death grip on the branch.

With her eyes half-shut against the sting of the foam and spray, Brittany watched the apparition of Jake start down the slope, somehow mastering the slick mud that had been her undoing. "Be careful!" she heard herself shout, then gave a hiccuping little laugh. Of *course* he would be careful! He was a product of her imagination, and she wouldn't *let* him do anything to get himself hurt!

But this imaginary Jake seemed to have a mind of his own. He wasn't careful at all. He splashed right into the water a few feet downriver of her and started wading upstream. "You're okay now, Brittany," he said, his voice thick. "Let go of the branch. The current will carry you straight to me, and I'll catch you."

Brittany wasn't sure. "Are you real?" she asked. "If you're not, I might let go and find you *aren't* there to catch me."

"I'm real and I'm here. I'll always be here for you, sweetheart." Jake grinned and held out his hands to her in an imploring gesture. "Come on, Kitten. Come to me so that I can tell you how much I love you."

A wave of emotion more powerful than anything the river had to offer swept over Brittany. But a part of her still wasn't convinced. It was all too perfect. Yet she heard herself say in a choked voice, "I'll hold you to that deal, Jake Mallory. I still don't know whether to believe in you, but I'm going to take a chance because . . . because I love you too much not to!"

With one deep breath and a little prayer for courage, she let go of the branch.

"Isn't this a lovely bed?" Brittany murmured as she snuggled against Jake in the four-poster where she'd felt so alone the night before. "The whole house is charming, and everything in it. Wait till you get a chance to look around. I just hate to see it sold. Especially this bed." She sighed contentedly. "It's wonderful."

"Wonderful," Jake agreed, pressing a kiss to the top of her head. "But a sleeping bag on the bare ground would be a patch of paradise as long as I had you in it with me, sweetheart."

She nuzzled her face into the hollow of his throat and shifted a little to correct the problem of the one tiny spot on her naked body that wasn't pressed against his, soaking up his body heat. He'd been holding her ever since he'd carried her back to the house, unceremoniously stripped off her clothes and his own, dried their shivering bodies with thick towels, and tumbled her into the bed and the cradle of his arms. "You're amazing," she said softly. "How can you be such a furnace when you were in that freezing water with me?"

"I wasn't there as long as you were," he answered. "Besides, it's my love that's warming you, not just my body."

Brittany smiled. Jake was keeping his part of their bargain. The instant his brawny arms had gone around her in the river, he'd started saying again and again how much he loved her. He hadn't stopped, and she wasn't tired of hearing it. She doubted that she would ever tire of hearing it. "If one person's love can warm another, you must be sweltering by now," she told him as she rubbed her cheek against his shoulder, still checking to make sure he was real.

His arms tightened, and he murmured the sweet words again.

After a very long time Brittany stirred, turning so

that her back was curved into Jake's front. "Time to warm the other side of me," she said with a smile.

He managed, with the help of his magic hands, to warm both sides.

"How did you know where to find me?" she asked, her voice ragged as her temperature began rising from warm to simmering.

Jake kissed the sensitive skin on the underside of her ear. "You weren't too difficult to track, Britt. Tiptoeing through the tulips isn't your style at the best of times. And you have great lungs." He hesitated before adding, "Besides, something happened to me in the car on the way here. I knew you were in trouble, or were about to be in trouble. I raced to get to you, but I was a little late."

Brittany went very still. "You mean . . . like a premonition?"

"I guess so, sweetheart." He nuzzled the side of her neck and glided his hand over her body to mold her even closer to him. "I'm beginning to think we must be soul mates, love. All the signs point to it."

"Soul mates," Brittany echoed softly. "I think you're right. Except that I had no inkling that you were on your way home. Why didn't you send me an extrasensory message?"

Running his finger tips over the slope of her thigh, Jake chuckled. "I wanted to surprise you, Kitten."

Kitten, she thought. The endearment wasn't necessary to ignite a desire that was already exploding inside her, demanding fulfillment. But it pushed her over the edge. She turned to face Jake, threaded her fingers through his hair, and pulled him down until their lips met. Her tongue delved into the hot recesses of his mouth, and her body pressed against him with sudden urgency.

Obliging as always, Jake rolled her onto her back

and moved over her, parting her thighs and completing the fused circle of their bodies.

This time, when they catapulted to the heights of ecstasy, it was with words of love tumbling over one another.

And afterward, when they both were sated and drowsy and utterly contented, Brittany pillowed her head on Jake's shoulder and decided there was something else she wanted to say before they slept. "It's ironic," she murmured, her fingers resting on the pelt of hair over his breastbone where she could feel the steady throb of his heartbeat. "The adventurer who flew off to the thick of an explosive situation had to race back to rescue the stay-at-home who'd gone out for a stroll in the woods." She walked two fingers up his chest, then tipped back her head to look at him as she touched his face, tracing the rugged features that had become so dear to her. "The last of my prejudices got knocked into a cocked hat today, Jake, just as you promised, along with the last remnant of my fear of loving you. I know now how crazy it is to try to second-guess the future. I also know there's no turning back for me. I'll go with you wherever you want me to, or I'll stay and wait for you if that's the way it has to be. But whatever happens, whatever choices you make, whether the future involves nest building or free flight, one thing won't change: I love you, Jake. All the way."

Jake's arms tightened around her, and sudden moisture filled his eyes as he gazed down at her in wonder. "Brittany," he said hoarsely, touching his lips to her fingertips, "there's so much I want to tell you. But first I need to ask one crucial thing. What about that independence you're so wary of compromising? Your conviction that no one can belong to anyone else?"

Brittany smiled, her own eyes filling with tears yet twinkling with sudden mischief. "Oh, that. Well, let me put it this way, Jake." She gave a nonchalant little shrug, then snuggled down to get ready for a long, sweet-dreaming sleep. "It's no big deal."

Holding her close, Jake hoped fervently that Brittany would feel the same way when she learned about all the plans he'd made for their future—without consulting her first.

Three days after Jake's return Brittany stood in the middle of the living room in his suite at the Somerset, staring first at him, then at Helena, then at him again. "Would one of you please repeat what I think I just heard?" she said, her heart hammering and her knees going weak. "Jake Mallory is *what*?"

"You didn't think you heard it, dear," Helena said with a complacent smile. "You did hear it. Jake Mallory is Garth Porter's replacement on my board of directors. What's more, I've insisted on giving him first option on buying enough of my shares to accumulate a majority when I decide to retire—which won't be for some time, now that I have the number-one Hotshot on my team."

Brittany shook her head as if trying to make the jumble inside click into place. "What happened to Garth?"

Jake was watching Brittany with worried intensity, all at once not sure she would be pleased with what he'd done, even when she got over her shock. He'd taken a lot upon himself. "Garth sold me his shares of course," he said carefully.

She blinked. "Oh, of course," she murmured, then gave her head another shake. "And why did Garth sell you his shares when he had his own plans for gaining a majority?"

"He had a couple of reasons. One was that Helena had already given me first option on her holdings. But you were another reason he was ready to take the money and run," Jake answered.

"*I* was? What do you mean?"

"Jake, let me explain," Helena put in. "Garth's father, Sam Porter, was a good man, but he and his wife were divorced, and Garth was raised by his mother—a manipulative, self-centered, grasping woman. Unfortunately Garth takes after her instead of his father. Ever since he inherited Sam's shares, he's been lobbying the other board members, doing his level best to form alliances against me. It hasn't worked. I've been blessed with incredibly loyal people."

"Maybe it's because you inspire loyalty," Jake pointed out, then returned his attention to Brittany. "Honey, when you flatly refused to consider the Santa Barbara job, Garth finally began to understand that the people around Helena would close ranks to protect her—including staff members who had nothing to do with Danforth Developments. So after I felt he'd had enough time to ponder his prospects for eventually becoming top dog in the company, I offered to buy out his shares. As I'd told Helena, I wanted to shake up my investment portfolio anyway. I wanted to put down roots, become part of something I believed in, build my own future instead of forever troubleshooting for other people's dreams."

Brittany made her way to the nearest chair and sank into it. "I can't absorb all this, It's . . ." She looked up at Jake. "Are you sure this is what you want, Jake?"

"I was never more sure of anything," he answered quietly.

She gazed up at him for several long moments. "You took quite a chance, didn't you?" she said at last.

"At first, yes." He paused, then went over to Brittany, hunkered down in front of her, and took both her hands in his. "When I first spoke to Helena about what I wanted to do, I wondered if I was taking too much for granted. I almost talked to you about it, but I knew it would work only if I was committed enough to make the decision on my own. By the time I presented Garth with my offer, I knew I was betting on a sure thing." He grinned. "Wasn't I?"

Brittany stared at him for another long moment, then pulled her hands from his, threw her arms around his neck, and kissed him with such enthusiasm, he rocked backward, lost his balance, and ended up on the floor with her eager body sprawled over him.

"Oh, my," he vaguely heard Helena say. "I do believe it's time I made tracks."

Twelve

After nodding and smiling and making faithful promises to Brittany's parents, to Casey and Alex, to Sandro and Trudy and the entire Hotshots team, and to just about everyone else at the wedding—including his own captivated mother and father—about how he would cherish the sweet, beautiful woman who was his bride, Jake could have kissed Ruby when he heard her say, "Now, see here, kiddo, Big Jake's a man who'll need plenty of tender, loving care and deserves it. See that you give it to him, hear?"

"I hear and I will," Brittany answered. She smiled at Jake as he stepped up beside her and slipped his arm around her waist. "Did *you* hear?"

"I did, Mrs. Mallory, and in the words of someone very close to me, I'm going to hold you to that promise." He'd never seen her more beautiful, he thought. His gaze took in the richness of her up-swept hair and the whimsical sprigs of tiny white flowers tucked into the soft waves; the creaminess of her skin, set off by the simple wedding dress of antique ivory satin and lace; the glow of happiness in her dark eyes.

He bent to kiss Brittany's upturned mouth, unable to resist and fired with the knowledge that he didn't have to resist. She was his wife. He loved that word: *wife*. His wife tasted of sweet champagne and warm, loving femininity, and he knew he couldn't wait much longer to steal her away to have her all to himself. "Have I told you lately that I love you?" he asked when he raised his head.

"Not for ages," Brittany murmured. "It's been at least fifteen minutes."

"Let me spirit you out of here, Kitten, and I'll make up for my neglect."

A surge of erotic warmth coursed through Brittany. She was eager to go with Jake, knowing he would have her purring all night long—and all the nights to come. She looked around at the gathering in Helena's luxurious penthouse suite in the Somerset. "The party seems to be in full swing," she observed, then gave Jake her most flirtatious smile. "I don't think we're needed here any longer. But where are we going?"

"To Fiji, remember?" Jake said with a teasing grin.

"You know what I mean, you beast. Our flight's not until tomorrow." Her voice turned husky as she asked, "Where are we going to stay tonight? You still haven't told me. I think Helena knows. She has that I've-got-a-lovely-secret look about her."

Jake was well aware of that look of Helena's. Every time he'd seen it, he'd felt a twinge of concern. Although he'd begun to have more confidence in Brittany's approval of decisions he'd made without discussing them with her, he knew that the one he was about to spring on her had better be the last. She wouldn't put up with many more surprises. But in this case he hadn't been able to resist. "You'll see, sweetheart," he said, holding out his hand to her.

Brittany smiled and placed her hand in his.

They made a quick tour of the room to thank their guests, paused long enough for Brittany to throw her bouquet—making certain Karen Blackwell caught it. She felt she owed the redhead something for having made the bad slo-pitch call that had triggered such a happy chain of events.

When at last they got away amid a flurry of good wishes, Brittany pestered Jake again about where they were going.

"Be patient, love," was his only answer.

It didn't take long for Brittany to guess their destination. As soon as Jake started driving along the coast highway toward Helena's house, she knew he must have made arrangements with Helena and the real estate agent to let them stay there for this one special night. "What a thoughtful idea," she said, reaching over to touch Jake's shoulder, thrilling to the fact that it was hers to lean on forever.

Even though the wedding dinner had been an early one, the sun had set by the time Jake and Brittany reached the house. But there were floodlights on the lawn, illuminating the impressive facade.

As Jake wheeled onto the driveway, Brittany noticed that the For Sale sign was gone. She felt a sad twist inside, a peculiar sense of loss. She didn't want strangers living in Helena and David's home.

Then Jake stopped the car, and Brittany's heart stopped with it. She stared at the new shrubbery hugging the stone walls. "Roses," she said, a catch in her voice. "Peach roses. Dear heaven, look at them."

Jake got out of the car and went around to help

Brittany out. She was dazed, not sure what to make of the flowers, not daring to hope. . . .

"I understand roses are perennials," Jake said, sliding his arms around her shoulders.

"Perennials?" Brittany echoed.

Taking a key from his pocket, Jake unlocked the door and pushed it open, then swept Brittany up in his arms. "Perennials, sweetheart. I think it means they're here to stay. I thought perhaps we should do the same, and maybe get started soon on another generation of Mallorys to tend them. What do you say, love?"

Finally letting herself believe, Brittany smiled up at Jake as he carried her over the threshold of their home. "Do you hear something ringing?" she asked softly.

"Yeah," Jake answered with a loving grin. "Your husband's biological clock just went off."

THE EDITOR'S CORNER

If there were a theme for next month's LOVESWEPTs, it might be "Pennies from Heaven," because in all six books something unexpected and wonderful seems to drop from above right into the lives of our heroes and heroines.

First, in **MELTDOWN,** LOVESWEPT #558, by new author Ruth Owen, a project that could mean a promotion at work falls into Chris Sheffield's lap. He'll work with Melanie Rollins on fine-tuning her superintelligent computer, Einstein, and together they'll reap the rewards. It's supposed to be strictly business between the handsome rogue and the brainy inventor, but then white-hot desire strikes like lightning. Don't miss this heartwarming story—and the humorous jive-talking, TV-shopping computer—from one of our New Faces of '92.

Troubles and thrills crash in on the heroine's vacation in Linda Cajio's **THE RELUCTANT PRINCE,** LOVESWEPT #559. A coup breaks out in the tiny country Emily Cooper is visiting, then she's kidnapped by a prince! Alex Kiros, who looks like any woman's dream of Prince Charming, has to get out of the country, and the only way is with Emily posing as his wife—a masquerade that has passionate results. Treat yourself to this wildly exciting, very touching romance from Linda.

Lynne Marie Bryant returns to LOVESWEPT with **SINGULAR ATTRACTION,** #560. And it's definitely singular how dashing fly-boy Devlin King swoops down from the skies, barely missing Kristi Bjornson's plane as he lands on an Alaskan lake. Worse, Kristi learns that Dev's family owns King Oil, the company she opposes in her work to save tundra swans. Rest assured, though, that Dev finds a way to mend their differences and claim her heart. This is pure romance set amid the wilderness beauty of the North. Welcome back, Lynne!

In **THE LAST WHITE KNIGHT** by Tami Hoag, LOVE-SWEPT #561, controversy descends on Horizon House, a halfway home for troubled girls. And like a golden-haired Sir Galahad, Senator Erik Gunther charges to the rescue, defending counselor Lynn Shaw's cause with compassion. Erik is the soul mate she's been looking for, but wouldn't a woman with her past tarnish his shining armor? Sexy and sensitive, **THE LAST WHITE KNIGHT** is one more superb love story from Tami.

The title of Glenna McReynolds's new LOVESWEPT, **A PIECE OF HEAVEN,** #562, gives you a clue as to how it fits into our theme. Tired of the rodeo circuit, Travis Cayou returns to the family ranch and thinks a piece of heaven must have fallen to earth when he sees the gorgeous new manager. Callie Michaels is exactly the kind of woman the six-feet-plus cowboy wants, but she's as skittish as a filly. Still, Travis knows just how to woo his shy love. . . . Glenna never fails to delight, and this vibrantly told story shows why.

Last, but never the least, is Doris Parmett with **FIERY ANGEL,** LOVESWEPT #563. When parachutist Roxy Harris tumbles out of the sky and into Dennis Jorden's arms, he knows that Fate has sent the lady just for him. But Roxy insists she has no time to tangle with temptation. Getting her to trade a lifetime of caution for reckless abandon in Dennis's arms means being persistent . . . and charming her socks off. **FIERY ANGEL** showcases Doris's delicious sense of humor and magic touch with the heart.

On sale this month from FANFARE are three fabulous novels and one exciting collection of short stories. Once again, *New York Times* bestselling author Amanda Quick returns to Regency England with **RAVISHED.** Sweeping from a cozy seaside village to the glittering ballrooms of fashionable London, this enthralling tale of a thoroughly mismatched couple poised to discover the rapture of love is Amanda Quick at her finest.

Three beloved romance authors combine their talents in **SOUTHERN NIGHTS,** an anthology of three original novellas that present the many faces of unexpected love. Here are *Summer Lightning* by Sandra Chastain, *Summer Heat* by Helen Mittermeyer, and *Summer Stranger* by Patricia Potter—stories that will make you shiver with the timeless passion of **SOUTHERN NIGHTS**.

In **THE PRINCESS** by Celia Brayfield, there is talk of what will be the wedding of the twentieth century. The groom is His Royal Highness, Prince Richard, wayward son of the House of Windsor. But who will be his bride? From Buckingham Palace to chilly Balmoral, **THE PRINCESS** is a fascinating look into the inner workings of British nobility.

The bestselling author of three highly praised novels, Ann Hood has fashioned an absorbing contemporary tale with **SOMETHING BLUE**. Rich in humor and wisdom, it tells the unforgettable story of three women navigating through the perils of romance, work, and friendship.

Also from Helen Mittermeyer is **THE PRINCESS OF THE VEIL,** on sale this month in the Doubleday hardcover edition. With this breathtakingly romantic tale of a Viking princess and a notorious Scottish chief, Helen makes an outstanding debut in historical romance.

Happy reading!

With warmest wishes,

Nita Taublib
Associate Publisher
LOVESWEPT and FANFARE

FANFARE

On Sale in June

RAVISHED

☐ 29316-8 $4.99/5.99 in Canada

by Amanda Quick

<u>New York Times</u> bestselling author

Sweeping from a cozy seaside village to glittering London, this enthralling tale of a thoroughly mismatched couple poised to discover the rapture of love is Amanda Quick at her finest.

THE PRINCESS

☐ 29836-4 $5.99

by Celia Brayfield

He is His Royal Highness, the Prince Richard, and wayward son of the House of Windsor. He has known many women, but only three understand him, and only one holds the key to unlock the mysteries of his heart

SOMETHING BLUE

☐ 29814-3 $5.99/6.99 in Canada

by Ann Hood

Author of SOMEWHERE OFF THE COAST OF MAINE

"An engaging, warmly old-fashioned story of the perils and endurance of romance, work, and friendship." -- <u>The Washington Post</u>

SOUTHERN NIGHTS

☐ 29815-1 $4.99/5.99 in Canada

**by Sandra Chastain,
Helen Mittermeyer, and Patricia Potter**

Sultry, caressing, magnolia-scented breezes. . .sudden, fierce thunderstorms. . .nights of beauty and enchantment. In three original novellas, favorite LOVESWEPT authors present the many faces of summer and unexpected love.

Look for these books at your bookstore or use this page to order.

☐ Please send me the books I have checked above. I am enclosing $ _____ (add $2.50 to cover postage and handling). Send check or money order, no cash or C. O. D.'s please.

Mr./ Ms. _____

Address _____

City/ State/ Zip _____

Send order to: Bantam Books, Dept. FN, 2451 S. Wolf Rd., Des Plaines, IL 60018

Allow four to six weeks for delivery.

Prices and availability subject to change without notice. FN 52 7/92

FANFARE

On Sale in AUGUST

A WHOLE NEW LIGHT

☐ 29783-X $5.99/6.99 in Canada
by Sandra Brown
<u>New York Times</u> bestselling author

Under the romantic skies of Acapulco, Cyn McCall and Worth Lansing succumb to blazing passion in one reckless moment, and must face the fears and doubts that threaten to shatter their new and fragile bond.

THUNDER ON THE PLAINS

☐ 29015-0 $5.99/6.99 in Canada
by Rosanne Bittner

"Emotional intensity and broad strokes of color...a strong historical saga and a powerful romance. Ms. Bittner [is] at the top of her form."
-- <u>Romantic Times</u>

INTIMATE STRANGERS

☐ 29519-5 $4.99/5.99 in Canada
by Alexandra Thorne

"Talented author Alexandra Thorne has written a complex and emotionally intense saga of reincarnation and time travel, where it just might be possible to correct the errors of time." -- <u>Romantic Times</u>

LIGHTNING

☐ 29070-3 $4.99/5.99 in Canada
by Patricia Potter

Their meeting was fated. Lauren Bradley was sent by Washington to sabotage Adrian Cabot's Confederate ship. He was sent by destiny to steal her heart. Together they are swept into passion's treacherous sea.

☐ Please send me the books I have checked above. I am enclosing $ _____ (add $2.50 to cover postage and handling). Send check or money order, no cash or C. O. D.'s please.

Mr./ Ms. _____

Address _____

City/ State/ Zip _____

Send order to: Bantam Books, Dept. FN, 2451 S. Wolf Rd., Des Plaines, IL 60018

Allow four to six weeks for delivery.

Prices and availability subject to change without notice.

THE SYMBOL OF GREAT WOMEN'S FICTION FROM BANTAM

Ask for these books at your local bookstore or use this page to order. FN 53 7/92

FANFARE

FANFARE

Rosanne Bittner

_____ 28599-8 EMBERS OF THE HEART . $4.50/5.50 in Canada
_____ 29033-9 IN THE SHADOW OF THE MOUNTAINS
                  $5.50/6.99 in Canada
_____ 28319-7 MONTANA WOMAN .... $4.50/5.50 in Canada
_____ 29014-2 SONG OF THE WOLF .... $4.99/5.99 in Canada

Deborah Smith

_____ 28759-1 THE BELOVED WOMAN .. $4.50/ 5.50 in Canada
_____ 29092-4 FOLLOW THE SUN .... $4.99/ 5.99 in Canada
_____ 29107-6 MIRACLE .... $4.50/ 5.50 in Canada

Tami Hoag

_____ 29053-3 MAGIC .... $3.99/4.99 in Canada

Dianne Edouard and Sandra Ware

_____ 28929-2 MORTAL SINS .... $4.99/5.99 in Canada

Kay Hooper

_____ 29256-0 THE MATCHMAKER, ... $4.50/5.50 in Canada
_____ 28953-5 STAR-CROSSED LOVERS .. $4.50/5.50 in Canada

Virginia Lynn

_____ 29257-9 CUTTER'S WOMAN, ... $4.50/4.50 in Canada
_____ 28622-6 RIVER'S DREAM, ... $3.95/4.95 in Canada

Patricia Potter

_____ 29071-1 LAWLESS .... $4.99/ 5.99 in Canada
_____ 29069-X RAINBOW .... $4.99/ 5.99 in Canada

Ask for these titles at your bookstore or use this page to order.

Please send me the books I have checked above. I am enclosing $ _____ (please add
$2.50 to cover postage and handling). Send check or money order, no cash or C. O. D.'s
please.

Mr./ Ms. _____

Address _____

City/ State/ Zip _____

Send order to: Bantam Books, Dept. FN, 414 East Golf Road, Des Plaines, IL 60016
Please allow four to six weeks for delivery.
Prices and availablity subject to change without notice.   FN 17 - 4/92